I AND SPROGGY

"Adam, who's ten, is dismayed when his mother tells him that his father is coming to New York to live, with his second wife (English) and her daughter, who needs his friendship. Adam's also a bit jealous when they do come and he sees how fond Dad seems to be of Sproggy, his stepdaughter. Anyway, how can he like a girl who's taller than he is, seems so self-confident, uses strange words, and—worst of all—appeals so much to his best friends that they invite her to join their all-boy club? . . . Greene has a sharp ear for dialogue and a sharp eye for children's problems; her style is fluent and natural, lightened by humor. Recommended."

—Bulletin for the Center for Children's Books

"Greene's masterful way with dialogue gives her story an easy flow, and her talent for dealing sensitively with situations that concern children is successfully employed."

—ALA Booklist, starred review

I AND SPROGGY

BOOKS BY CONSTANCE C. GREENE

A Girl Called Al
The Unmaking of Rabbit
Isabelle the Itch
Isabelle Shows Her Stuff
Isabelle and Little Orphan Frannie
I Know You, Al
Beat the Turtle Drum
I and Sproggy
Your Old Pal, Al
Dotty's Suitcase
Double-Dare O'Toole
Al(exandra) the Great
Just Plain Al
Star Shine
Al's Blind Date

I AND SPROGGY

CONSTANCE C. GREENE

ILLUSTRATED BY EMILY McCULLY

Puffin Books

To Schuyler and Thayer
  the nicest little girls
  I know

PUFFIN BOOKS
Published by the Penguin Group
Viking Penguin, a division of Penguin Books USA Inc.,
375 Hudson Street, New York, New York 10014, U.S.A.
Penguin Books Ltd, 27 Wrights Lane, London W8 5TZ, England
Penguin Books Australia Ltd, Ringwood, Victoria, Australia
Penguin Books Canada Ltd, 2801 John Street, Markham, Ontario, Canada L3R 1B4
Penguin Books (N.Z.) Ltd, 182–190 Wairau Road, Auckland 10, New Zealand

Penguin Books Ltd, Registered Offices: Harmondsworth, Middlesex, England

First published in the United States of America by The Viking Press 1978
Published in Puffin Books 1990
10 9 8 7 6 5 4 3 2 1
Copyright © Constance C. Greene, 1978
All rights reserved
Poem on page 95 reprinted by permission of G.P. Putnam's Sons from *Here,
There and Everywhere* by Dorothy Aldis. Copyright 1927, 1928 by Dorothy Aldis.
LIBRARY OF CONGRESS CATALOGING IN PUBLICATION DATA
Greene, Constance C.   I and Sproggy / by Constance C. Greene ;
illustrated by Emily McCully.   p. cm.
   Summary: The meeting between an eleven-year-old boy and Sproggy,
his English step-sister who comes to New York City, is less than
idyllic, but time, events, and other people help to change their relationship.
   ISBN 0-14-034542-6
   [1. Brothers and sisters—Fiction.   2. New York (N.Y.)—Fiction.]
I. McCully, Emily, ill.   II. Title.
[PZ7.G8287Iab 1990]   [Fic]—dc20   90-33722

Printed in the United States of America
Set in Times Roman

CHAPTER 1

It was a slow, hot Saturday in September. Heat shimmered in the shadows. Boats pushed their way through the oil slick coating the river. The leaves on the trees lining East Eighty-eighth Street lay limp and exhausted in the breathless air.

Adam decided to walk over to Gracie Mansion to see what was going on. With any luck at all, the Mayor might be having a party. Adam had rubbernecked at many of the parties the Mayor of New York threw at Gracie Mansion. Generally speaking, they looked as if, as Charlie would say, a fun-filled time was being had by all. Charlie was not only the handyman in Adam's apartment house, but also Adam's friend. Adam planned to attend some of the functions at the Mayor's when he was a celebrity. It was necessary to be someone special to get an invitation. The Mayor didn't fool around with just anyone.

The place looked closed. No sleek black limousines disgorged famous folks, no striped tents set up on the lawn rang with music and laughter. The guard at the mansion's entrance, ordinarily a cheerful sort, looked surly.

"Nothing going on, huh?" Adam said.

The guard shrugged. "Everybody's at the ocean or lolling around their swimming pool," he said. "What's the matter with you?"

"Lost my water wings," Adam said and went on his way.

The park was as bad. Two old ladies who might have been twins, dressed in identical lavender pants suits which matched the color of their hair, sat on a bench, pigeon-toed, bulging shopping bags clutched to their bosoms like life preservers, elbows sharp and vigilant against marauders.

"I don't care what his IQ is," one said angrily. "He's dumb. To me, he's dumb."

"You can't say that," the other protested.

"I just did," came the reply.

It might have turned into a fight worth hanging around for, but Adam doubted it.

As a last resort, he headed for home. He lived between York and First avenues with his mother and their dog, Rosalie. On a day like this the lobby of their apartment building wasn't a bad place to be. It was gray, nothing but gray. Gray walls, gray floor, gray curtains. A lady on five who said she was an interior decorator had volunteered her services for nothing.

"I figure that's about what they're worth," a thin, haughty person from 3-C had sniffed when she got a look.

Every time Adam walked into that lobby he felt as if he were walking into a dense fog, a sensation he sometimes enjoyed. When Charlie saw the new decorations, he said, "It's like a blinking British pea souper, that's what." Charlie had been stationed in England during World War II and knew about English fogs.

Charlie had wavy gray hair, bright blue eyes, and large hands and feet. "When I was a kid," he'd told Adam, "they got in my way. Didn't grow into 'em until I was a man." And up until last week Charlie had had sideburns. He'd spent some time growing them to please his wife Millie. On the day they were complete, he'd shaved them off. "Every time I got a look at them burns out of the corner of my eye," he'd confided to Adam, "I felt like I was being followed. Millie like to have cried."

As Adam opened the apartment-house door, Charlie was down on his hands and knees, searching diligently for discarded cigarette butts. Charlie himself had given up smoking a year ago January 18. He didn't miss it except with his morning coffee, he'd told Adam more than once.

"People are such slobs," Charlie said when he caught sight of Adam. "It's on days like this I wish I was the Shah of Iran."

Adam sat down cross-legged on the cool floor.

"Why?" he asked.

"That guy has it made. You ever see his uniform? Gold braid, medals, ribbons that won't quit. Plus money and power." Charlie sighed. "Moola. The guy has it all. But all the medals and gold braid in the world isn't going to do any good without the moola. I understand the Shah eats off gold plates and wears diamonds in his teeth."

Adam frowned. "I don't think that's such a hot idea," he said irritably. "Suppose he forgets and takes out his teeth at night the way my grandmother does. What then?"

"I don't know. What?" Charlie asked, sitting back on his heels.

"Once my grandmother got up in the middle of the night when she was staying with us and almost drank her own teeth. She was thirsty and it was dark and she forgot where she'd put them and she almost swallowed them. That was close. She remembered just in time, just as they were going down. Otherwise she might've had a problem. How would it have looked in the newspaper? WOMAN STRANGLES ON OWN TEETH. That might've been very embarrassing for my mother if that'd happened.''

"Not to mention your grandmother," Charlie said with feeling.

"It's on days like this that I wish I was the Bionic Man," Adam said. "I'm practicing walking in slow motion. I'm getting pretty good. Want to see me?"

But Charlie got up and wielded his broom slowly, lazily, like a man sweeping sand off a beach and into the ocean.

"The Bionic Man is here today, gone tomorrow," he said. "The Shah is forever. When the old man passes on, his son takes over. They never run out of Shahs in Iran. It's that generation thing that counts."

Charlie had often boasted that he never missed reading *The Wall Street Journal*. That and the eleven-o'clock news, he'd said, were what raised him up from the rest of the crowd, opened up his mind to new ideas, made him different from your ordinary, everyday person.

"You want to see the generation thing, stick around," Adam said.

"How so?"

"My father's coming tomorrow," Adam said gloomily, staring at his shoes.

"Hey, what's the long face for?" Charlie asked. "I call that an occasion. What you looking so sour for?"

"It's great that my father's coming," Adam said. "I haven't seen him for almost two years, you know. It's just that he's bringing his new wife and her kid."

"Is that right?" Charlie said, smiling. "It sounds like a festive, fun-filled time will be had by all. All of you getting together like that. No hard feelings between your mom and dad. One big happy family. You're a lucky boy, Adam. You get a nice little step-sibling in the bargain. What kind did you get, a boy or a girl?"

"It's a girl," Adam said glumly. "She's English."

"I figured as much," Charlie said, "seeing as how you told me your daddy married an English lady. It's music to my ears, the way those folks talk. Soothing, it is. Maybe with the new air fares me and my wife Millie can swing a trip to the U.K. next year. My wife Millie's never been there. I can taste the fish and chips now." Charlie smacked his lips.

"You won't catch me hanging around when they get here," Adam said. "I'm splitting."

"What's got into you? What kind of talk is that?" Charlie sounded sore. "You got a nice little stepsister coming all the way across the ocean and you take off. What kind of thing is that?"

"It's easy for you to say," Adam told him. "How'd you like it? A total stranger practically related to you and everything coming to your house and you have to be polite and act like everything's peachy when it isn't? That's not the easiest thing in the world, Charlie. Put

yourself in my shoes. It's darn tough. I'm not sticking around here, that's for sure."

He got up and stalked around the lobby. "I thought, you being my friend and all, you'd understand. But you don't."

Charlie laid his huge hand on Adam's shoulder.

"I'm trying, kid," he said. "I'm also thinking about your dad. Thinking about how he'd feel if you take off when you know he's coming to visit. You can't do that to your poor old daddy, Adam."

"He's not old," Adam said indignantly. "He's nowhere near as old as you are, Charlie."

"I never told you how old I was," Charlie said, drawing back. "I never."

"Once you said, 'Guess how old I am,' " Adam reminded him, "and I said, 'About forty-five or fifty, I guess,' and you got sore because you weren't that old. So I guess you're about, oh, around thirty, maybe?" Adam didn't want to offend Charlie a second time.

"You think I look about thirty, eh?" Adam could tell Charlie was pleased. He knew Charlie was vain about his physique. In his youth he'd been a light heavyweight boxer, and he stayed in shape by lifting weights, working out at a gym, and jogging in the park on his day off.

"O.K., Charlie." Adam gave in. "I'll stick around to see my father, but that's all."

"You're all heart, kid," Charlie said, spitting on the doorknob, giving it an extra shine. "All heart."

CHAPTER 2

"What'd you say that girl's name was?" Adam asked his mother. He noticed with pleasure that in his new shoes he was almost as tall as she was in her sneakers.

"Sproggy," she said.

"That's not a name!" Adam protested. "I never heard it before. Did you?"

"No," she said. "But just because neither of us has heard it doesn't mean it isn't a name. Anyway, it's probably just a nickname."

Rosalie inched her way over to Adam, tongue hanging out. She hated the heat worse than anyone else. To make her happy, he rubbed behind her ears.

When Adam had been small and Rosalie a puppy, he'd shaved off part of her fur with his father's electric razor. Luckily for Rosalie, his father had come into the bathroom just in time to save her from instant baldness.

"She's off her feed today," his mother said, scooping out yolks of hard-boiled eggs into a bowl. "Hasn't eaten a thing all day. Her nose is out of joint."

"She heard somebody named Sproggy was coming over. That's enough to put anyone's nose out of joint," Adam said.

Why couldn't her name be Jane or Sally or Susan? He knew girls by those names. There were three Susans in his class alone. Although as far as he was concerned, all three of them could go jump in the lake. He would have been happy to hold them underwater for a while.

"If there's one thing I can't stand," Adam told Rosalie, "it's a dog who sulks." Rosie stared at him, pretending she didn't know him, pretending he wasn't there.

"I do hope this isn't a mistake." Adam's mother sighed. "This getting together. Sometimes I get carried away."

"Yes," Adam agreed, "you do." Without warning, his thoughts flashed back to the night four years ago when his father and mother had told him they were getting a divorce. He had been six, almost seven. He could see the three of them sitting in the living room, windows open to let in a breath of air. It had been this same time of year and very hot. The sound of taxi horns bleating and a fire truck going by had been very loud.

His father, standing straight, unmoving, hands behind his back, had said, "Your mother and I are getting a divorce. We want you to know, Adam, it has nothing to do with you."

He knew lots of kids whose parents were divorced. The thought that he might have had anything to do with the divorce would never have occurred to him, but it interested him that his father said that.

"It has nothing to do with anyone but us," his father continued. His mother, he remembered, had worn a pink dress and a faint, faraway smile. She almost never wore a dress. It must be an occasion.

"We think it would be better if we lived apart. As it happens, I have to go to England for my magazine for a couple of years, so this seemed like a good time."

A good time?

"What's the matter?" Adam had asked. Even now, after all that time, he could hear himself say, "Do you have a girl friend?" He knew a kid whose father had a few girl friends.

That was the only time in his life Adam had seen his father blush. He didn't know fathers *did* blush. The color rose from his father's neck into his face and made him look younger than usual.

"No," he'd said in even tones, "I don't have a girl friend. Your mother is still my friend and you are my child and I love you very much.'' He didn't say, ''I love you both very much.'' He'd said, ''I love you,'' meaning Adam.

''That's O.K., Dad,'' Adam had told him, watching his mother's face. Her eyes glittered and she nodded, as if in agreement. She left the room then, and Adam and his father had sat quietly, eyeing each other, not talking, listening to the street noises.

He'd gone to visit his father in England once. Two years ago he'd flown the Atlantic by himself except for a blond stewardess who was supposed to look out for him, see he got off at the right stop. She had paid much more attention to the man sitting next to him, though. The man had asked her if she'd ever been a model or in the movies. She didn't look like any movie person to Adam, and he'd examined her very carefully after the man went to the lavatory.

''Buzz off, sonny,'' the stewardess had hissed out of the corner of her mouth as the man came back down the aisle. Adam spent the rest of his trip looking out at the darkness, figuring out how he'd inflate his life raft if the plane had to ditch in the ocean, wondering what his chances were for tripping up the stewardess as she went back and forth. He would have liked to have caught her with a full tray. Like so many of his plans, it didn't work out.

''How come you and Dad are still friends?'' Adam asked now. ''If you're such big friends, why didn't you

14-

stay married?'' That had always puzzled him.

She wiped her hands on the sides of her pants. ''I told you, Adam. I like your father. As a matter of fact, I like him better now that we're divorced than I did when we were married. We make better friends than we did lovers, you might say.''

She closed her eyes and, clasping her hands in front of her, sang a song about being just friends and lovers no more that made Adam wince at the silly words.

She opened her eyes. ''That's all I can remember. My mother's uncle used to play that on the piano when I was a little girl.''

''Nobody would listen to that kind of junk these days,'' Adam said in a sour tone.

''You've got to be kidding,'' she said. ''Some of the junk I hear nowadays makes that sound like Shakespeare.''

Then she hugged him. ''Our marriage wasn't a total loss, though. I got you out of it.''

He didn't mind her hugging him. He liked it. But, ''You didn't answer my question,'' he said, pulling away. ''If you like Dad so much, why didn't you stay married?''

She considered. ''I don't really know,'' she said finally. ''We fell out of love, I guess. People fall in love and, if they're lucky, they stay that way. It doesn't always happen, though.''

''Now that Dad got married again, does that mean

that you might too?'' Adam asked. Harry Carter took her to the theater and other places. Once he'd taken Adam, just the two of them, to the Central Park zoo on Sunday. Harry was all right. There was just one thing. He hadn't known what an aardvark was. Adam forgave him, but he felt, in his heart, that his father would have recognized an aardvark immediately.

Other than that lapse, though, Harry was all right.

''Your father's new wife is named Arabella,'' Adam's mother said, pursing her lips as if she hadn't heard his question. ''Very English, that. Don't much care for it myself, but then the English have different ideas. They like their toast cold and their mustard hot. Maybe it comes from owning India all those years. Who knows?''

''Mom,'' Adam said patiently, ''I asked you a question.''

''Yes, you did. Well, I'm thinking.'' She looked at him a long time.

''Not without checking with you first, I wouldn't,'' she said.

''You wouldn't have to do *that*,'' he said, although he thought privately that it would be a good idea. ''How old did you say she was?''

He couldn't bring himself to say that name. He also knew the answer, but it was like biting down on a sore tooth. He wanted to make it hurt again and again.

''Two months older than you. They're thinking of

sending her to your school if they find an apartment near us."

"If she was only a boy," Adam said, lying down on the floor next to Rosalie, putting his cheek against the cool linoleum. "A boy about two years younger than me. Then if the kid looked at me cross-eyed, I'd work him around the head and shoulders."

"What a lovely, kindhearted, charitable boy you are," his mother said. "It warms the cockles of my heart to hear you."

Rosalie sniffed at Adam. Her moods were subject to rapid change. She licked him fondly. Adam sat up.

"You have bad breath," he told her. "You have such halitosis it's a wonder you have any friends."

"You'll hurt her feelings," his mother said. "Poor Rosie." She patted her. "If only you could talk you could tell him off."

"I think she can talk. I think she talks to herself at night when we're asleep. I bet she has a big, deep voice."

"Oh, no," his mother said. "I imagine her voice is high and dainty, like a lady at a tea party. 'Will you have one lump or two?' " his mother said, imitating Rosie's voice. They both laughed. Rosalie went out to the living room and lay under the couch. She knew who they were laughing at.

"Should we have cole slaw or potato salad?" Adam's mother asked. "Or both?"

"Both," he said.

"All right. Would you run down to the corner and get me a half pint of cream for the dessert?" She gave him a dollar.

Adam lifted his feet inch by inch, as if a brick were tied to each shoe. The Bionic Man had taken over. Keeping his elbows close to his sides, lifting his feet high and slow, he left the building and crossed the street. The heck with Sproggy. If he concentrated on perfecting his Bionic Man imitation, she and all other mortals would fall before his superior power. The world would be his. The wind rushed through his hair as he raised his chin and made his eyes mere slits to cut down on any fallout particles. A taxi rounded the corner and nearly nailed him. The driver leaned on his horn and shouted. Adam made it to the store all right. Then he had to get change for the dollar to call home and ask his mother what it was she'd sent him for in the first place.

CHAPTER 3

"Dad called," Adam's mother said when he returned with the cream. "He wants to take you out for dinner and maybe a movie tonight." He followed her into her bedroom.

"How come? If he's coming over tomorrow, how come he wants to take me out tonight?" Adam asked. "Who else is going?" If *she* was coming along, he'd stay home.

"Just the two of you. I guess he wants to see you alone so you can talk. He said to tell you he'd go to any movie you want except one with blood and violence in it. He said he doesn't care about you—you're young and strong and can take that kind of thing. But he can't stand the sight of blood in living color. He always did have a weak stomach," she said fondly. "That and the back of his neck were what attracted me to him in the first place."

She leaned over and brushed her hair until it crackled. "And it works out very well," she said, "because Harry's taking me to the ballet." When she finished brushing, she dipped her finger into a pot of blue and traced the color on her eyelids. He watched, fascinated, as she put smudges of red on her cheekbones, rubbing the color into her skin. Then she darkened her lashes with mascara.

"I am nothing if not a natural beauty," she said. He liked her better without all that stuff on her face.

"Do you think it would be gilding the lily if I put these on?"

She held up the pair of earrings that Adam's father had given her when Adam was born. They were like a hummingbird's wing, lacy and golden, and Adam loved them more than any other piece of jewelry he'd ever seen.

He sometimes imagined the scene in which his father had presented them to her. There he lay in his mother's arms, his face all squinched and red and furrowed like a newly plowed field. There he was, with both of them looking down at him with such love in their faces that their features were blurred. He had a picture of the three

20-

of them that someone had taken right after they'd brought him home from the hospital. It seemed to Adam that the bundle in his mother's arms resembled nothing human, but was more like a troll they'd found under a bridge somewhere. As for his parents, he almost didn't recognize them in the picture—they looked so young and foolish.

She took off her sneakers and put on a pair of shoes with straps and heels. When she stood up, she seemed to have grown several inches.

Adam hoped very much his mother would put on the earrings now. He would never say so. Not in a million years. She had to do it on her own. If she wore them, even if it was when she was going out with Harry Carter, it seemed to him she was donning a part of her life when there had been him, her, and his father. A part of her life that was gone but still there.

"I bet Dad would never give Arabella a pair of earrings like those," he said.

"No." She screwed one into her ear. "No, I don't expect he would."

Adam's father and Harry arrived on the same elevator. "Hi, Dad," said Adam, as if he'd seen his father only last week.

His father caught him in a bear hug, smashing Adam's nose against his jacket. He wouldn't have minded staying there awhile.

"My Lord, but you're getting big!" he said. "I guess that's to be expected in two years, though."

"You look great, Dad." Adam returned the compliment, pleased that his father thought he'd grown.

"Getting a little thin on top," his father said ruefully, smoothing his hair, "but otherwise no complaints." Adam recalled that his father had the hair in his family. His grandfather and two uncles looked like Kojak. Baldness was hereditary, Adam knew. He figured he didn't stand a chance. If he didn't start growing, really growing, and soon, he'd probably start losing his hair when he hit high school, and by the time he graduated, he'd look like a bald midget. The thought was not appealing.

Harry ran his fingers through his thick dark hair and smiled at them. Adam was glad to note that, although Harry was taller, his father's shoulders were broader.

"There you are." His mother appeared, looking very pretty. Why not? She'd spent enough time at it. Too much, Adam thought, no matter what the results. "I see you two have met. Good to see you, Dick." She gave Adam's father both her hands as if they didn't belong to her and she wasn't sure what to do with them. He took them in his.

"You look marvelous," he said. She laughed and they stood for a moment as if they were alone.

Adam noticed she laughed more than usual, that her eyes shone and she made fluttery motions with her

hands, tossed her hair back from her face with a twist of
her head, and, in general, was behaving strangely. He
wasn't at all sure he liked it. He secretly considered her
appearance extremely interesting, even spacy looking.
She was an illustrator, a painter of pictures, a lady who
could almost sit on her own hair. Ordinarily, he was
proud of her. Now he felt she was being somewhat un-
dignified. As he watched her out of the corner of his
eye, she seemed to become more animated every minute.

"You're more beautiful than ever," Adam's father
told her. That didn't help to calm her down any.

Harry stood around clearing his throat. Finally she
noticed him.

"Harry dear," she said, laying her hand on Harry's
arm—which Adam felt to be completely unnecessary,
"we must be off or we'll miss our curtain. You won't
be late, you two, will you?" she asked coquettishly.
Adam felt like saying, "Hey, Ma, pull yourself
together," but he didn't.

On the way to the restaurant, Adam was tempted to
show his father how well he was able to walk in slow
motion but decided he'd save that for later, after they
got better acquainted. He liked walking down the street
beside his father. He kept hoping someone he knew
would pass by, do a double-take, and exclaim, "You
two are the image of each other! I'd have known you
were father and son anywhere!" No one did.

"Good evening, sir." The waiter greeted them. "A table for two?" What did he think they wanted, a table for six? Adam wondered. They sat down, and he flipped open his big linen napkin and laid it across his legs, the way his father had done.

"The *escargots* are very good tonight," the waiter said. "Also the *moules*."

"*Escargots* are snails," his father explained, "and *moules* are mussels."

"Muscles?" Adam asked, incredulous.

"Yes, mussels," his father replied.

After a lot of thought, Adam said, "Do you have any hamburgers?" The waiter looked as if he'd been seized with gas pains.

"How about the *pot au feu*?" Adam's father said. "It's like stew and very good." Adam reluctantly agreed. You had to watch your step in a joint like this, he thought, or they might slip something really weird at you.

After the waiter had taken their order and left them, Adam and his father smiled at each other like two strangers on a bus who had caught each other's eye. It was like the night his father had told him about the divorce. They sat quietly while the noises swirled around them, saying nothing, thinking private thoughts. Two years is a long time. A quarter of Adam's lifetime, he figured. He was good at math.

"How are things at the office?" he finally asked his father.

"Fine, fine," his father said absentmindedly. Adam broke a piece of bread in half, buttered it, and chewed slowly, thinking about what to say next. He remembered to chew with his mouth closed. His mother would have been proud.

"I wanted to talk to you about something," his father said.

"Dad," Adam said, "about this girl."

"That's what I wanted to talk to you about." His father looked relieved. "Sproggy is her name. She's your age. A nice kid, really, You'll like her. I think. In any event, I'd like you to more or less take her under your wing. Show her the ropes, be kind to her. Can you do that for me? I'm very fond of Sproggy."

Do you love her more than me? Adam wanted to ask. And didn't. Instead he said, "I don't know. That's a lot of things. Why does she have that dopey name?"

"Oh, it's one of those things that begins in childhood and then sticks, I guess."

The waiter brought their dinner. "Everything all right, sir?" he asked.

"Everything's fine, thank you."

The waiter went away.

"You might think, when you meet her, that Sproggy's not in need of any looking after. She seems very grown-up, very much in charge." His father began to eat. Adam did the same. The *pot au feu* was pretty good. He was glad he hadn't had hamburger. You had to be adventurous once in a while if you wanted to get anywhere in life, he decided.

"But she's really *not* so grown-up, and I think she could use a friend. I told Arabella I was going to ask this favor of you, Adam." His father extracted a snail from its shell and said, "Would you like to try one?"

Adam shook his head. He wasn't *that* adventurous.

"We'd both feel much better about Sproggy if we knew you'd look out for her at first," his father said. "I've told Arabella so much about you. We'd be grateful if you'd keep an eye on her for a couple of weeks."

"I'll try, Dad," Adam said. I don't want to, he thought. I wish Dad hadn't asked me. "I don't think I can do much, though," he said.

"Well, thanks. That's a relief."

They finished their dinner. "How about some dessert?" his father asked.

"I'm full," Adam said. It was all that bread.

"You can't manage a confection of whipped cream and chocolate?"

The waiter presented Adam with just such a confection, and he demolished it.

"That's a little soldier. I knew you could do it." The check arrived, and Adam watched as his father piled bills in a heap on the tray. All that for one meal.

"Are you up to a movie?"

"Mom said you couldn't take any blood and violence," Adam said. "That sort of limits us."

"Have you ever seen Charlie Chaplin?"

"No," Adam said.

"That's good. This will be your first exposure." They walked a few blocks and saw *The Gold Rush*.

"It was the best movie I ever saw," Adam said as they walked home. "Wait'll I tell Kenny and Steve what they're missing."

He thanked his father for a great time. "See you tomorrow," he said. "It was the best." That night Adam dreamed he was walking up the steps of Gracie Mansion. The windows were lit and music was playing. When he got inside, the Mayor, a little man with a mustache, dressed in a black suit and a derby, and carrying a cane, greeted him.

CHAPTER 4

"How come we're using napkins that have to be ironed?" Adam asked next morning. "Instead of paper ones?"

"Use your head," his mother said. "One doesn't use paper napkins at a time like this."

He thought of asking, "Why?" and decided against it.

"I might have to leave after lunch," he said. "I and Kenny have a date."

She grasped him by the shoulder. For a small woman she was pretty strong.

"Now you listen to me," she said from between tight lips. "There'll be no skinning out of this one."

She surveyed the table critically. "It'll have to do," she said. The doorbell rang. She jumped. Adam froze.

"That's them," he whispered.

His mother arranged a smile on her face.

"Look pleasant," she snapped. Rosalie caught the vibes and tiptoed into Adam's room and under his bed.

"Lucky little creep," he said to himself, wishing he could join her.

"Hello, hello," Adam's father cried as they opened the door. Adam crouched behind his mother, glad for the first time in his life that he was small.

His mother murmured, "So glad. Delighted. And this must be—"

"I'm Arabella," the tall thin lady said to Adam, grasping his hand in hers. Her fingers were long and dry. It was like shaking hands with a spider, Adam thought.

"And this is Sproggy," Adam's father said, putting his arm around Sproggy. "Darling," he said to her, "this is Adam!" The grownups stood in a half circle, smiling down at the little ones getting to know each other. He never called me darling, Adam thought.

"How simply super to meet you!" Sproggy said cheerfully. Adam kept his hands behind his back so she couldn't get hold of him. If she did, he felt, there was no telling what might happen.

Sproggy was arrayed in a sea of blue denim. Denim jacket, denim shoes, blue jeans, even a denim backpack. Her hair was orange. She seemed to him a formidable older woman.

"It's perfectly charming of you to have us," Arabella said. "We've so been looking forward to meeting you all."

Adam's mother smiled and passed the nuts. "And do have a deviled egg," she said. "Adam." He passed the deviled eggs. Either they or the plate were slippery because one landed smack in the middle of the rug. Yolk side up, fortunately. "No harm done," Sproggy said, picking it up and popping it in her mouth. His mother laughed delightedly.

If *I* had done that, Adam thought.

They discussed the weather, and the city, which they found fascinating, and the high cost of everything.

"Very pricey, that," Arabella kept saying. "But Dick and I," she said, "are so pleased with how nicely Sproggy's been settling in. Aren't we, darling?" she asked Adam's father.

All eyes, including Adam's, turned on Sproggy, who was rooting around in her backpack. "Do you play chess?" she asked Adam. "I've just learned, and I'm awfully keen on it."

Adam didn't play.

"What a pity," Sproggy said.

"Adam dear," his mother said, "will you give me a hand for a minute?"

"I don't care what you say," he complained when

they were out of earshot, "she's not my age. She's a teen-ager. I bet she's a teen-ager."

"Girls grow faster than boys up to a point," his mother said, taking things out of the oven.

"Ma," Adam said, "please. Just let's get this over with, all right?"

"Mummy sent me in to ask if I might help," Sproggy said at the kitchen door. She got to carry in the rolls. Adam burned his hand on a casserole dish. Everyone allowed as how they'd never had such a delicious lunch.

"It's time for Rosalie's walk," Adam said after the table had been cleared. He avoided his mother's eye and made a complicated business of fastening the dog's leash to her collar.

"What a dear little dog," Sproggy said, patting Rosalie. One thing Rosie couldn't stand was to have a stranger touch her. She began to wheeze. In moments of stress Rosalie frequently developed asthma.

"Why don't you take Sproggy with you?" Adam's father suggested. "Show her around."

"Give me a break, Dad," Adam wanted to say. And didn't.

"That would be lovely," Arabella agreed. "Just don't stay out too long, though. I have heaps of things to do."

Sproggy stood beside him in the elevator. She was half a head taller than he. Easily. Maybe more.

"How old are you?" he said.

-31

"I'll be eleven next month," she said. "I understand you'll be eleven in December."

"Who told you?"

"Daddy."

"My father?"

"Yes. He said I might call him that. I hope you don't mind?" she asked, and when he didn't respond she smiled at him. The elevator came to a stop in the lobby. The door slid open. Adam started out. Unfortunately, Sproggy must've believed in ladies' being first because she walked out too. They collided in the doorway. And Adam tripped on Rosalie's leash and fell in a heap.

"Oh, I say, that's my fault," Sproggy said and helped him up. "I'm frightfully clumsy, I'm afraid." Her cheeks were red with embarrassment.

"Hey," Kenny said, watching, "I was just coming up to see you."

"Well, I'm not there," Adam said crossly. He felt humiliated that Kenny had caught her picking him off the floor as if he'd been a piece of string. Rosalie's wheezing increased.

Adam charged toward the street; the others followed. "Who are you?" he heard Kenny ask Sproggy.

"I'm Sproggy," she said. "And you?"

"I'm a friend of Adam's. Kenny's the name."

"I'm very glad to meet you, Kenny. I say, does he always walk this fast?"

"Only when someone's chasing him. Hey, Adam," Kenny called, "where's the fire?"

They waited at the corner for the light to change.

"That's Sproggy," Adam said to Kenny. "From England. My father's new wife's kid."

"No kidding. You ever been to Westminster Abbey?" Kenny asked her.

"Heaps of times," Sproggy said.

"That's where I wanted to go. To walk on all those famous people buried there. Kings and queens and poets. If my father could've scratched up the bread, I and Adam would've gone there to visit his father." Kenny was a pessimist. He wore a doleful look as comfortably as if it were a suit of old and well-loved clothes. "If one of my sisters was planning to go to Westminster Abbey," he said, "she'd get there. Not me. I got gypped. I usually do."

"Bread?" Sproggy looked puzzled.

"He means money," Adam said.

They walked toward the park. "Steve's calling a meeting of the club tomorrow, second bench from the river," Kenny said, out of the side of his mouth. "If it doesn't rain or a tornado doesn't show up or anything. Pass it on."

"Who do I pass it on to?" Adam asked. "It's just you and me and him in the club."

"I know," Kenny said. "I like to say, 'Pass it on.' "

Sproggy looked from Adam to Kenny. "You boys sound a bit bonkers to me," she said.

"Listen," Kenny said, "I haven't got much time. My mother's on the warpath. She says if we're not all home in time for Sunday dinner, it's the last one she's cooking. I've got to split. Keep the faith." He extended his fist in a farewell salute and took off.

"I say, he's jolly nice even if a bit strange," Sproggy said. "Is he your best friend?"

"I and Kenny have been friends all our lives," Adam said, exaggerating some. They had met in kindergarten when Kenny had pulled out Adam's chair from under him. Adam had punched Kenny in the nose, and it started to bleed. That had made them best friends and blood brothers.

"My best friend's name is Wendy," Sproggy said. "I miss her frightfully. We write to each other once a week, but it doesn't take the place of being able to see her and have a good natter."

Adam took the park steps two at a time. Rosie kept up, and Sproggy, even with her backpack, was just behind.

"You don't realize how much you're going to miss a person until they're not around," Sproggy said.

"I guess," Adam replied. He remembered how he'd missed his father.

"We seem to be the only people out for a walk,"

Sproggy said. "It's not like London. There'd be masses of people out in London."

"It's going to rain. That's why. Isn't that right, Rosie?"

"In London it's always about to rain," Sproggy said.

"Got the time?" The question came from a lean, pale, scruffy youth who'd popped up from nowhere.

"I don't have a watch," Adam said. He knew that routine. Give 'em the time and they'd rip off your watch in nothing flat.

"Hello," Sproggy said. "Are you another friend of Adam's?"

"Sure," the boy said. "And I'll be even friendlier if you kids hand over the bread. I've got a knife in my pocket," he warned, coming so close Adam could smell him. He smelled of fried pork chops and dirty underwear. "I don't want to hurt you, so hand it over."

"He means money," Sproggy said.

"No kidding," Adam snapped.

He turned out his empty pockets. He never had any money.

"How about you, lady?" the boy asked Sproggy.

"I've got some but it's not your kind, I'm afraid." She dove into her backpack and came up with some English money. "You're welcome to it," she said, "but it won't do you much good."

The boy looked at it carefully, swore, and tossed it in the bushes. "I guess I'll have to settle for the pooch, then," he said. "She might be worth a couple of bucks to somebody."

He wasn't getting Rosie. Don't struggle, his mother had often told Adam. Hand over what they want. Your safety is the important thing.

This smelly rat wasn't getting Rosie.

"Get lost!" Adam shouted to Sproggy. He snatched up the dog and ran. He saw Sproggy swing her pack at the mugger, getting him in the back of the neck. The guy fell, clutching his head.

They ran toward Gracie Mansion. There was always a guard there. Lungs bursting, hearts pounding, scared, they ran.

"There's a bobby," Sproggy said breathlessly, coming to a halt outside the fence surrounding the house. They peered through at the long black limousine letting people out at the foot of the steps.

"Let's tell him what happened," Sproggy said. "Maybe they could catch him."

Adam looked behind. "It's O.K., he didn't follow us. Maybe you killed him." Boy, Dad should be here now, he thought. Who's taking care of who? What a joke!

Sproggy looked alarmed. "Oh, I don't think so," she said. "He was only stunned."

A man and woman came out of the mansion and stood at the foot of the steps, greeting their guests.

"That's the Mayor," Adam said. "And those others

are big shots. You have to be a big shot to go there."

"He looks a jolly sort," Sproggy said approvingly. They pressed their faces against the fence, even Rosie, and watched.

"I think New York is simply ripping," Sproggy said happily. "Nothing this exciting ever happened to me at home."

CHAPTER 5

During the night a terrific thunderstorm woke Adam. Rosalie crawled in beside him, quivering. Maybe King Kong was out there, looking for a juicy kid or two, Adam thought.

Peering out the window, he saw nothing but lightning. Thunder rumbled, rain wet his face. He looked down, half hoping to see Kong lurching down the middle of the street, trampling taxis under his massive feet. Chin on hands, Adam savored the thought that he was the only boy awake in the entire city.

It was a good thing Sproggy had kept her mouth shut about the mugger. That was all Adam's mother would have needed to hear. If she'd found out about that guy, she'd probably chain Adam to his bed and let him travel only as far as the bathroom by himself. He had enough problems as it was. Ten was a tough age, as far as he was concerned. Too young to be on your own, do what you wanted when you felt like it, and too old to sit around watching TV, munching animal crackers. Maybe eleven would be better.

If only I was taller, Adam thought. He was worried about being the shortest kid in his class. Ever since he could remember, he'd had that dubious distinction. Last year, for one glorious moment, another boy had been even smaller. Then it turned out the kid was so smart he was transferred to the sixth grade. The final insult.

Once he'd had a dream in which he was the same size he'd been in second grade. The other kids kept growing and growing and he stayed the same. They reached down and patted him on the head and talked baby talk to him. It had been horribly real.

It was cool having his father back in town, within walking distance. I and my father, he thought, gazing out into the rain, will go to ball games and the Museum of Modern Art whenever we want. I and my father will be a team.

Arabella was like a stork, he thought, standing on her long, thin legs. A nice stork. But Sproggy was more like a dinosaur. She mowed things down in her path. They were not at all alike, Arabella and Sproggy.

Hair brushed against his arm, masses of bristly hair. Panic seized him. King Kong *was* out there in the vast darkness, making the air boil, ready to reach in and pluck him and Rosalie out like olives from a jar and carry them both off to his lair, a secret place where no other human had ever been. There Adam would spend the rest of his days combing the tangles out of Kong's ears and cooking huge dishes of tiger stew sprinkled with dragon's dung. Rosalie's chore would be to lick the dishes clean.

"Cut it out," Adam said to her crossly as she rubbed against him. "You are such a chicken."

After the guests had gone that afternoon, Adam had asked his mother, "How'd you like them?"

"Um," she said, lighting a cigarette. She smoked rarely. "They're very nice," she said.

She didn't even inhale. He could have given her a couple of tips, learned from Kenny. Kenny's brother had taught him, and he'd passed it along. Smoking was foul, Adam thought. And it stopped you from growing.

Now Rosalie crept closer. In disgust, Adam went back to bed, letting her fight her way across the pitch-black room and under the sheet, whimpering. Ordinarily Adam, who sometimes had a kind heart, would've talked her back with "It's O.K., Rosie, it's O.K."

Let her figure it out for herself. Big baby.

In the morning the air was fresh and clear, the sky a piercing blue, and the terrible heat had gone. Adam cooked himself an egg and, to make amends, added another to the pan for Rosalie. She liked hers sunny-side up. It was the least he could do after he'd been so mean.

"There you go," Adam said in a placating voice, putting her breakfast on the floor. "Just the way you like it."

Rosalie gave him the cold shoulder. She had been known to hold a grudge for days. He began to read the newspaper. She sidled up to her plate, sniffed, and, without wagging her tail in gratitude, licked discreetly at her egg, her tongue barely emerging from her mouth. If she had to eat, she was not going to let him know she was enjoying herself.

The doorbell rang and Adam went to answer it. His mother, he knew, was locked in her study, working on some illustrations that were due next week. She was not to be disturbed except for an emergency.

Sproggy stood there, armed with her backpack, still in her denim ensemble.

"Did you sleep in that?" Adam asked sourly.

There was a silence while she looked him over. "Americans have such an odd sense of humor," she said finally. "It takes some getting used to. I expect I shall, eventually." But she looked extremely doubtful.

"Mummy sent me over to say thanks for a lovely time yesterday," she said. "May I come in?" she asked, coming in. "Mummy also said I should ask you and your mum to our flat for tea. We're having scones and trifle."

"Your flat?" One thing at a time. What were scones and trifle? He wanted to know, but he'd be darned if he'd ask *her*.

"Yes, our flat. We've borrowed it from a friend of Mummy's. It's just 'round the corner."

If the flat was 'round the corner, no matter what it was, that was too close for comfort.

Sproggy peered into the living room.

"I didn't say anything," she announced proudly. "About yesterday, I mean. About you-know-what. About that bloke in the park."

"You want a medal?"

"A medal? What a ridiculous idea," Sproggy said in an unnaturally high voice. He glared at her and, to his dismay, saw her eyes were wet.

"It's just an expression," he said against his will. "You don't have to take everything I say so seriously."

"I thought when I came to America I wouldn't have any difficulty with the language," she said, wiping her face with a handkerchief. "I guess I was wrong. I don't understand half of what you say."

Adam was undecided. If he shut the front door, he'd shut her inside with him. Also, that would mean she was going to stay awhile. On the other hand, he couldn't just stand there in his pajamas.

In his pajamas.

He bolted for his bedroom and slammed the door, locking it.

"I say, Adam," she said through the crack, "you *are* odd. You lunge about so."

He didn't answer. If she thought he'd gone back to sleep, she'd leave. On the other hand, the possibility was good that she'd sit down, relax, take her chess set out of her backpack, and play a game against herself, waiting for him. He wouldn't put it past her.

She'd probably win, too.

He put his ear to the crack and heard nothing. Maybe she'd gone. He was on the verge of unlocking the door to investigate when she called, "I say, Adam, may I use your loo?"

That was close. He'd almost been trapped a second time.

"We don't have one," he hollered back. What was a loo?

"You don't have one? How very strange," Sproggy said. She was outside the door, he knew, waiting to pounce. She hadn't budged. She was going to wait all day until he had to come out and have dinner. He could hear his mother say, "Won't you stay and have dinner with us, dear?"

She'd stay. He knew she would.

"In a nice flat like this you don't have a loo?" Sproggy asked. "Not even one?"

"You'd better go home and get one," he told her.

Sproggy laughed. She laughed a long time. Adam got madder and madder. She was laughing *at* him. He knew it. Laughter had a special sound when it was directed *at* you.

"A loo is a toilet," she finally said, when she'd had her fun. "A lavatory. You don't get one, you use one. Fancy that." She began to laugh again. Adam put his pillow around his head.

"Fancy that, he doesn't even know what a loo is," Sproggy said in a clear voice which penetrated the pillow. "Just fancy that."

The front door slammed. Adam lay back on his bed, his hands behind his head, thinking. Life was suddenly very complicated, it seemed to him. Only a couple of days ago his mother and he and Rosalie had been a unit. He had missed his father, but he had become used to missing him, even deriving a certain amount of pleasure out of it. Now his father was virtually around the corner, complete with a new family.

You shouldn't have asked me to take care of her, Dad, he said in his head. You had no business. You look out for her. She's your responsibility, not mine. You brought her here. Now you take over. So what if I didn't know what "loo" means? It's a dumb word. She laughed at me because I didn't know her word. She has a nerve.

If I laughed at her every time she didn't understand what I say, I'd probably sound like a baboon. Adam got up and stood on his head, then got to his feet, flared his nostrils and scratched his chest, making noises like a baboon he'd seen on a nature program.

The doorknob rattled.

"Adam," his mother called, "what's going on in there?"

He unlocked his door.

"Ma," he said, "please don't disturb me. I was in the loo practicing being a baboon."

"Oh. Well, don't forget to brush your teeth, change your underwear, and empty the wastebasket." She went back down the hall and into her study.

And Adam went back to stand watching himself, perfecting his imitation. No telling when it might come in handy.

CHAPTER 6

"Well, how'd it go?" Charlie asked Adam later on that day.

"How'd what go?" Adam said, knowing what Charlie meant.

"The little girl from across the sea. Your English step-sis. My wife Millie says you're some lucky boy to have a sis from foreign shores. Millie's mom and dad were from the other side, too, you know."

"What other side?"

"Scotland, Germany, Ireland, all those. Millie says she's polyglot. I frankly had to look it up," Charlie said. "Millie's very well-read. Give her a word, she'll tell you what it means like that." Charlie snapped his fingers. "She does that crossword puzzle in jig time. That's the wonderful thing about this country of ours."

"The crossword puzzle?"

"Everybody's from someplace else." Charlie got back to his original subject. "Every American citizen has blood from other places running in his veins. What's your ethnic background, kid?"

"I haven't got one," Adam said.

"Sure you do. You got to have one," Charlie insisted. "Everybody has an ethnic background. Now mine, it's part Russian, part Swedish, with a little Polish thrown in for good measure. That's where I got this nose." He turned his profile for Adam to get the full effect of his nose.

"Some people, they'd have a nose job if they had one like mine," he said proudly. "Not me. It's my heritage. How'd you get on with your new relatives?"

"All right," Adam said shortly. Maybe sometime he'd tell Charlie about yesterday. Not now.

"Mr. Early was looking for you," Charlie said.

Mr. Early lived alone with only his parrot for company in a tiny apartment on the top floor. Two years ago his wife had died, and last year Mr. Early had had a mild stroke. "All by himself," Charlie had told people, "with the TV going and water boiling away in his teakettle, he keeled over. If I hadn't gone up to check on a plugged drain, Mr. Early might've gone to his Maker.

"They got the little fella just in time," Charlie said. "Five more minutes and the jig would've been up." Charlie always referred to Mr. Early as "the little fella" because Mr. Early was a very small man, a little taller than Adam, not as tall as Kenny or Sproggy. His wife had towered over him.

"The little fella's better off," Charlie said. "God rest her soul, he's better off. She bossed the daylights out of him. Wouldn't let him put on his galoshes without telling him how. Couldn't call himself his own. A big woman she was, with a sharp tongue."

But Mr. Early seemed to miss her. Maybe he liked being bossed.

"Just the man I'm looking for," Mr. Early said, coming in from the street. His white hair grew in little wisps all over his head. He looked like an ancient baby, Adam thought. A very good-natured, very old baby.

"Got a job for you. Pays good money," he said with a sly wink at Charlie. They both knew Adam's weakness for ready cash. "One dollar per diem."

Adam didn't know what "per diem" meant, but he liked the sound of "one dollar." Maybe he'd have to rob a bank, hold someone hostage for that kind of dough. Never mind. He was up to it.

"What's 'per diem' mean?" he asked.

"It means 'per day,' " Mr. Early said. "When I was your age, I'd have known what it meant. At least I think I would. You had any Latin or Greek?"

"No," said Adam, "I'm barely into English."

"That I believe," Mr. Early said. "That I believe."

"What do I have to do?" Adam asked.

"Feed Burton," Mr. Early said. Adam remembered Burton. He was Mr. Early's parrot, a surly bird of nasty disposition and moldy tail feathers. A bird who imitated everything he heard. "He was a great companion for my Ida," Mr. Early told Adam. "They watched the soap operas every afternoon. Burton knows all the parts."

Now that Mrs. Early was no longer around, Mr. Early told Adam, he turned on the soaps just to make Burton feel the old days were back.

Last time Adam had gone to Mr. Early's apartment to sell him some Girl Scout cookies (which Mr. Early had refused, saying Adam didn't look like any danged Girl Scout to him), Burton had screeched from the next room, "Oh, no! Not that kid again!" So naturally Adam didn't have a warm spot in his heart for Burton.

Still, a dollar was a dollar.

"I'm going to visit my sister in Jersey for a few days," Mr. Early said. "She's my younger sister but everyone takes her for my older sister. She's had a hard life. But not any harder than mine, come to think of it.

"You want to know why I'm so fit?" he asked suddenly.

Adam nodded.

Mr. Early paused. "It's all those innards I eat. Keep me young, they do."

"Innards?" Adam said.

"Yep. Liver, kidneys, brains, that kind of thing." Mr. Early smacked his lips. "My sister's a very good cook, but she and my wife never did see eye to eye. Ida was a very positive person," he said. "Not everyone likes a positive person. But now she's gone, bless her, and so I go to my sister's and she fixes me calf's liver and onions, with a fried banana on top. Or brains in black butter, or kidney stew. Oh, my, I can taste them now."

So could Adam. He concentrated on the ceiling, humming loudly. He was astounded. He had never heard of such food. Just thinking about the things Mr. Early had described, seeing them in his mind no matter how hard he tried to keep them out, made him feel queasy.

"The animal's innards are the best thing for man to eat," Mr. Early went on, turning to Charlie and oblivious to Adam's discomfort. "They're chock-full of food value, not to mention vitamins. You take your vitamins now. People going out, spending vast amounts of money on bottles of vitamin pills. Why, if they bought a nice piece of calf's liver, that's all the vitamins they'd need. Not like your hamburgers and your junk food." He turned back to Adam. "Try innards, young man. If you want to live to be healthy, wealthy, and old, that's the ticket."

"About Burton," Adam managed to say. "What do I feed him?"

"He's big on grapes—old grapes. I don't buy the really fresh stuff. He doesn't know the difference. Then there's special seeds he eats at night, seeds I send away for. They're like innards for him, keep him in good shape. He needs fresh water once a day and clean newspapers in his cage every morning. Think you can handle it? Is it a deal?"

"It's a deal." They shook on it.

"I'll be going Wednesday morning, coming back Saturday, maybe Sunday. I'll give you the key to my apartment. And one more thing," Mr. Early said, "if it's not too much trouble, could you come up when *All My Children* is on? Turn on the set for him?"

"What's *All My Children*?"

"It was my wife's favorite soap opera," Mr. Early said, looking a little sheepish. "They watched it together, and he misses it. I know it sounds crazy, but if he sees ten, fifteen minutes of *All My Children* every day, he's a new man. The sadder it is, the better he likes it. Makes him know his life isn't all that bad. Not compared to those folks, it isn't. He's like a person, Burton is," Mr. Early finished proudly.

"I'll come up later so you can show me what to do," Adam said.

"Good idea. He's very particular," Mr. Early said. "Wants things just so. Got that from Ida, I expect."

Twirling his cane, Mr. Early marched into the elevator. When he'd gone, Charlie shook his head in admiration. "He's a great old boy, that's for sure. Don't know how he puts up with that parrot, though. He's a bossy old bird. Takes after . . ."

"I know," Adam said. "Ida."

"We must speak well of the dead," Charlie said in a pious voice.

"You said it, not me," Adam said.

The back buzzer sounded, and while Charlie went to answer it, Adam glumly contemplated his lot. He'd promised his father to look out for Sproggy. That was a laugh. She should be looking out for him. She'd picked him up like a feather after she'd knocked him down, and she'd rescued him from a mugger. What would she do next? She's a red-haired Mafioso, he thought. A red-haired Mafioso who plays chess. What's more, he didn't even have an ethnic background. Some days it didn't pay to get out of bed, he decided.

"Three-C," Charlie said succinctly. "Would you believe it's their TV set this time? 'You're so clever, Charlie,' she says, 'you can fix anything.' " He did an imitation of Mrs. 3-C's voice. "What she means is, she don't want to call the serviceman, he charges ten, fifteen dollars just to look at *her*, never mind the TV. You know what I told her?" Charlie chortled. "I told her my wife Millie's religion prevents her from having TV in the house, so I'm not familiar with the workings of a

TV set. That really racked her back. She says, 'What, pray tell, is her religion?' and I had all I could do to keep from exploding.''

"What *is* her religion?''

"Sometimes you got no sense of humor, Adam,'' Charlie said. "Sometimes you disappoint me, pal. When does school open?''

"Please.'' Adam sighed deeply. "Don't remind me. Next week, that's when.''

"Education is the key,'' Charlie intoned. "Look at me. Thirteen when I quit school, and here I am, a handyman. I'm thinking of going to school nights to improve myself. I respect education. An educated man I also respect. Me and my wife Millie are both thinking of going to night school. Next thing you know we'll be big shots. Who knows?''

"There you are, Adam.'' A voice pierced Adam's eardrums. "Jolly good.''

Charlie said, "This is the little girl from across the briny, eh what? Cheerio and pleased to meet you. I'm Charlie.''

Sproggy shook Charlie's hand. "How super!'' she said.

"No, the super's Mr. Courtney,'' Charlie said. "I'm only the handyman.''

"I meant it was super to meet you,'' she explained. "In American that means, I think, terrific.''

"Oh,'' Charlie said. "Sure. It's jolly super to meet

you, too." He smiled at Adam. He was certainly getting into the swing of things fast, Adam thought.

"I've got to go," he said. "I and the boys are having a club meeting."

"May I come?" Sproggy asked.

"It's a private club," Adam said. "No outsiders allowed. Plus," he said, scowling, "no girls. Especially no girls. We made a pact."

"You are a very old-fashioned chap, I think," Sproggy said with asperity. "The world has changed. As you Americans would say, 'Get with it!' Good-bye, Charlie. It was nice to have met you," Sproggy said. "I shall see you again soon, I hope."

"Come over any time," Charlie said. "I'd be pleased to see you. Always got time for a limey," he said. "No offense."

"Righto, Yank," Sproggy said and went on her way.

"You're rude," Charlie said when she'd gone. "You were very rude, Adam. I'm surprised at you. And disappointed. Why do you want to be so short with her? She meant no harm."

"My father wants me to take care of her," Adam said. "Can you see me taking care of her? That's ridiculous."

"You mean because she's bigger than you or what? Just because she's big doesn't mean she's not timid inside, coming to a strange country, going to a new school, getting used to all the things that are different here. Put yourself in her shoes, kid," Charlie said.

"They'd be miles too big," Adam said with a long face. "My father had no business asking me to do that. He had no business."

"Aha!" Charlie said. "That's it. You don't want to share your father with her. Is that the trouble?"

"I don't care about that," Adam said in a lofty tone. "He's my father, not hers. She hasn't got a father."

"Everybody's got a father," Charlie said. "The smallest fish in the sea, the biggest camel in the desert. You know about the facts of life?" Charlie peered intently at Adam.

"Oh, boy." Adam sighed. "I'm not up for a lecture on the facts of life, Charlie. My mother filled me in on that stuff a couple of years ago. I'm not sure I buy everything she said, but yeah, I know all about it. We had it in science class, too. But don't tell me my father's her father, because he isn't."

"I get it," Charlie said. "Now I get it. Your trouble is you're not used to sharing. You don't know how to share your daddy because you never had to." Charlie pointed a finger at him. "Being an only child, you had him all to yourself. And your mother, too. Now we got a little outlander moving into the picture, and you're in a snit. I wouldn't have thought it of you, kid." Charlie shook his head. "I'm disappointed in you, Adam, and that's for good and sure."

All right. There was just enough truth in what Charlie

said to make Adam smart a little from his words. He'd never especially minded being an only child. There were plenty of pluses about it, like being the center of things, not having to share stuff. Kenny, for instance, and Steve Skully, they were always complaining about not being able to have a new bike or a new this or that because there wasn't enough money to go around; the other kids in the family needed something more important. Braces or glasses, dumb stuff like that.

Last time Steve's mother and father had gone out, they'd left his oldest brother in charge. Steve's younger brother, aged eight, had written a list of all the mean things they'd done to him.

"Stuck finger at nose four times," the list had read. "Said, 'You little faggot,' five times, hit me on head with *Fortune* magazine twice." When Steve's father got a load of the list, he'd lowered the boom. No TV for a week, no treats, all privileges cut off.

"If you can't behave more responsibly than that," Steve's father had told him and his older brother, "you don't deserve any extras."

And Kenny reported the same stuff. He was always getting into trouble for things he did to his siblings. At least Adam didn't have to cope with that kind of business. And up until now, up until Sproggy had entered his life, Charlie and he had never had an angry word. They'd been friends. They'd admired each other. O.K. She'd spoiled that.

"So long," Adam said coolly, tucking in his shirt. "I've gotta go to the park for our meeting. I'll see you, Charlie."

"Sure." Charlie squirted cleaner on the window and rubbed it with a cloth as if his whole career depended on getting it clean. "I know how it is. You got friends waiting, you gotta go. Don't keep them waiting, kid. Go along and have a good time."

"It's not a good-time thing," Adam said. "It's a club meeting. We have to decide all kinds of things."

For a minute Charlie left off polishing. He looked hard at Adam. "Right," he said. "A club is a serious business. I know. I been in clubs. A very serious business they are. Take it easy."

He turned his back to Adam and went to work again, whistling.

CHAPTER 7

Adam took the long way around to Carl Schurz Park. He walked up First Avenue to Ninetieth Street, then cut across to York and down to Eighty-fourth, lifting his feet high, looking in windows. Then he ran across Eighty-fourth to East End Avenue and up two blocks to the park entrance. Kenny and Steve were sitting on the bench, waiting for him.

"You ever hear of a guy named Dickens?" Kenny asked as Adam sat down, winded.

"Who's he play for?" Adam said.

"The Rangers," Steve said in his positive way. "I'm pretty sure it's the Rangers."

"He doesn't play for anyone," Kenny said. "He writes books."

"Oh," the others said. "That."

"My sister was reading this book he wrote," Kenny said, "and at the same identical minute she was reading, there was the story on the tube. They were acting out his book on the tube. I couldn't get over it." Kenny shook his head. "There it was in color and everything. And she was reading that book when she could have seen it on the tube."

The three boys sat and contemplated the wonder, the strangeness of it all.

"Let's get down to business," Steve said. He was club president because the club had been his idea. His father was on Wall Street. He got a lot of hot tips on stocks. Steve even had a share of stock his father had given him for his birthday. His mother was a lawyer. Steve often figured out loud that that made him a whiz, a mini-money man, a fifth-grade tycoon. He spent a lot of time banging his gavel and hollering, "Come to order!"

Adam was vice-president. He decided on fund-raising activities and kept track of infractions of the rules. So far they hadn't had any of either.

Kenny was treasurer. He held the financial reins and held them tightly.

"I'm getting bored," Adam said. He was irritated

because of what Charlie'd said. "Nothing ever happens in this club."

"I think we should increase the dues to fifteen cents a week," Kenny said. "That way we can buy a new soccer ball sooner."

"I can't afford it," Adam said. "If you increase the dues, I'm getting out."

"Out!" Kenny rolled his eyes. "Out of the club? Outrageous! You can't do that, Adam. That'd leave us with only two members. You can't have a club with two members."

"I'm not red-hot on soccer. I thought this was going to be a club to make money."

"Soccer is very big and bound to get bigger," Steve said. "My father says so." Adam was getting pretty fed up with hearing words of wisdom from Steve's father. He and Kenny began to argue.

"Come to order!" Steve shouted, banging his gavel.

A woman sitting on the next bench said in a loud voice, "Children should be seen and not heard." Then she turned to her friend and said, "My daughter's boyfriend is into life insurance."

Adam eavesdropped. He picked up a lot of things that way. Besides, let Kenny and Steve argue. He was tired.

"What's *that* mean?" the other woman said.

"He's a life-insurance salesman. That's what they say these days. Into. Everything's into."

"Tell her to hook up with a dentist or a doctor, that's where the money is," the other woman advised.

They got up and strolled away.

"I vote we take a karate course," Adam said. "My father knows a man who can break a board with his bare hands, he's so strong from taking karate. He practices on his steering wheel while he's driving."

"That guy must rack up a lot of cars that way," Kenny said. "Bounces them off telephone poles, causes traffic jams, accidents. Maybe knocked off a couple of people even. Crazy." He and Steve shook their heads some more.

"I think this club stinks," Adam said.

"What's the matter with you?" Kenny said. "You act like you just stepped into a hornet's nest."

"None of your business," Adam said. "If you can't get something started, we might as well forget the whole stupid club."

A silence fell, as thick as smoke.

"Hey!" Kenny cried. "That looks like Rosalie over there."

"Where?" Adam said.

"Right there." Kenny pointed. It did look a lot like Rosie, but it couldn't be. It also looked a lot like . . .

"I can't stand it," Adam said. "I can not stand it."

"Hi, Sproggy," Kenny called.

"There you are." Sproggy waved and walked toward them. "I offered to take your dog for a walk, and your

mum said that would be fine. Now she's used to me. Aren't you, Rosie?'' She bent down and patted Rosie on her nose.

"Nobody calls her Rosie except me," Adam said in a cold voice. "Her name's Rosalie."

Rosalie turned her big brown eyes toward Sproggy and wiggled her rump with pleasure. She even sat on Sproggy's shoes, something she did only when she loved someone. She didn't sit on just anyone's shoes. Only Adam's and, once in a great while, his mother's or Charlie's. It was a sign of approval when Rosie sat on your shoes.

"Shape up," Adam said. "Shape up, you dog."

Very deliberately, Rosie adjusted her position so that she, too, had turned her back on Adam. First Charlie, now Rosie. What was this, anyway? What was happening?

"I thought Rosalie didn't take to strangers," Kenny said.

"I'm not a stranger," Sproggy said. "I'm practically one of the family."

The bad temper that had been plaguing Adam all day took charge.

"That's what you think," he said in a peevish tone. He got up. "When you guys make up your minds about what kind of club this is, let me know." He stuffed his hands in his pockets and made his way toward Gracie

Mansion. He pretended he'd been invited to a party there that would start in a few minutes.

"Yes, sir," the guard would say, recognizing Adam. "Just go right in, sir. They're expecting you." And Adam would climb the stairs to the front door. When he reached the top, the door would open, the Mayor would come out, shake hands with Adam, and say, "You're just in time. We were waiting for you."

Only as Adam came to the guard's booth, peered in, and said, "Hi. How are things today?" the face turned to him was an unfamiliar one. A new man who didn't mess around, apparently. A sour guard who hated kids.

"Move along there," he told Adam in a rude voice. "Just you move along and don't bother me."

Adam went home and lay down on his bed.

CHAPTER 8

He stared at the orange and yellow clowns and circus animals cavorting on the walls. Ridiculous. He was almost eleven. What did they think he was, an infant? Charlie thought he was a rat. He thumped around on his mattress for a while, digging the heels of his shoes deep into it, then he put his feet deliberately on the paper and began to walk up the wall with a heavy tread, as if he were a man weighing two hundred pounds.

Now even Rosie liked her. Rosie sat on her feet and turned her back on him. As Charlie also had.

Adam hoped his mother would hear him and holler at him for putting his dirty shoes on the wall. He wanted her to holler at him, but he couldn't say exactly why.

Charlie was wrong. He didn't care if he had to share his father with Sproggy. Not even if he was just getting to know his father all over again. He didn't care.

You lie, a voice said in his head. You lie.

Adam put his hands behind his back and pretended his legs were in chains. No. His hands were chained behind him and his feet were his only tools to freedom. He was being held captive in a dungeon surrounded by a moat filled with alligators. It was a situation that called for tremendous courage and ingenuity. As he thrashed about, struggling to free himself, almost overcome by the stupor of despair, his mother said, "What on earth are you doing?"

She stood in the doorway. "I thought Big Foot had broken his way into the place while you were gone." She sat down beside him. "I was just thinking, Adam, you'll need new clothes for school. Why don't we go shopping this afternoon? We should have gone last week, but somehow we always put things off until the last minute."

"I don't," Adam said. "You do."

"We're running out of time. School starts next week. O.K. If I get to work and stay at it until about two-thirty, we can go then."

"Where's Rosie?" Adam asked. He knew the answer.

"Sproggy took her for a walk," his mother said.

"Rosalie seemed glad to go. She doesn't get enough exercise as it is."

"I have to go up to Mr. Early's to get instructions for feeding Burton," Adam told her. "That's his parrot. Mr. Early's paying me a dollar per diem to feed him while he goes to visit his sister in Jersey."

"At those rates, I'll be able to borrow money from you for a change," she told him. "I'll get back to work now."

Somewhat comforted, Adam put his feet back on the wall, his hands still in chains. The snapping jaws of the alligators formed an ominous ring around him. It was all he could do to stay out of their way, loose his bonds, and figure out a way to be friends with Charlie again.

CHAPTER 9

Adam could hear the TV going when he went up to Mr. Early's. That must be the old bird watching his soaps. "Good boy," Mr. Early said, answering his ring. "I told Burton you'd show up. He's waiting for you."

I bet, Adam thought. I just bet.

"Oh, no!" Burton shouted, right on cue. "Not that kid again!"

"Behave," Mr. Early said but in a tone Adam felt was far too gentle. That parrot needed to be put in his place. It was up to him, Adam, to do the job. It seemed wise, however, to wait until Mr. Early had gone off to Jersey to eat innards.

"Here are the seeds and the clean newspapers for his cage," Mr. Early said, showing Adam around. "Wash out his water dish every day and I'll leave you the money for the grapes. And you won't forget the TV?"

"You can trust me," Adam said. He looked around Mr. Early's apartment. It was very neat and clean and sunny. The table was set for one. "Always set my table for dinner right after I finish lunch," he said. "That way I know I have something to look forward to."

Suddenly he said, "I decided last night what to do with my body."

"Your body?" Adam said, startled.

"After I die. I woke at precisely three a.m. I usually do. It's a terrible time to sit by yourself and think," Mr. Early said. "But there it is. Old people wake up in the middle of the night. Don't know why. Don't need so much sleep, I guess. Anyway, everything seems pretty grim at three a.m., so I decided I better think positive thoughts. And I decided to give my body to science. They might be glad to get it." He chuckled. "My brain and eyes ought to be worth something even if I did have a stroke. Now my heart's a different matter. The old ticker isn't in such good shape, but those doctors might find some use for it. The brain is O.K. Good's it ever was, if I do say so. Don't like to brag," he said, "but it's true."

Adam thought that was a cool idea. He decided he'd

leave his body to science, too. Of course, they might turn it down. But he figured that would be *their* tough luck.

"You want your money now or later?" Mr. Early said.

"Well," said Adam, "I'd rather have it now. On the other hand, I'd spend it before I even did my job. Better pay me when you get back," he said reluctantly.

The bell rang. Mr. Early went to answer it.

"I say." Sproggy's voice rang out. "Is Adam here?"

"Come in, come in," Mr. Early said. "Any friend of Adam's is a friend of mine. Haven't had so many visitors in a month of Sundays."

"She's not my friend, she's my stepsister," Adam said.

"What a beautiful parrot," Sproggy said. Burton was quiet, studying her.

"We had a parrot named Pete at home. He was clever. Parrots are very clever, very smart," she said. Burton smirked.

"What do *you* want?" Adam asked Sproggy. He couldn't believe she'd followed him here. "I'm arranging a business deal," he told her. "I and Mr. Early are talking business."

"I wanted to know if you'd like to go to the pizza parlor with me," Sproggy said. "Mummy gave me enough money to treat you, if you like."

Pizza. How long since he'd had a pepperoni pizza?

The juices started to flow in Adam's mouth. He could not only smell the pizza, he could taste it.

"I can't," he said. "I've got to go with my mother to get new clothes."

"If I were a spot younger, my dear," Mr. Early said gallantly, "I'd go with you. But pizza, dear me, no. Have you been in America long?"

"A week and a day," Sproggy said. "I'm quite liking it, although I don't understand the language completely yet."

"The last time I was in London, my dear wife and I walked through Hyde Park," Mr. Early said. "It was a beautiful day after a week of rain, and there was a rainbow. I'll always remember that rainbow."

"Quite." Sproggy nodded. "Hyde Park is the most beautiful park in the whole world. Where is your wife? I should like to meet her."

"She passed away two years ago," Mr. Early said, as if he'd said it many times and was beginning to get used to the sound. "She passed away on the fourth of February. February is a good month for dying, it seems. Both my dear mother and father died in February, although not, of course, in the same year."

"How terrible!" Sproggy said. "I'm so sorry."

If I don't get out of here, Adam thought, I might kill her. If I could figure out a way, I would. Why did she have to ask Mr. Early about his wife? It might make him feel bad all over again.

But Mr. Early smiled at them both. "That was a long time ago," he said.

"I have to go," Adam said. "See you, Mr. Early." As fast as he moved, Sproggy kept up. He ran down the stairs, not wanting to wait for the elevator. She was right behind him.

Outside his door he stopped.

"You are such a nerd!" he hollered at Sproggy. "You are such a super nerd it hurts my gut!"

"We don't have nerds in England," Sproggy said in a cold voice.

"A nerd has furry warts all over it, and it makes disgusting noises and smells like chicken manure." He pinched his nose closed with his fingers so when he talked he sounded as if he had a terrible cold. "And if you ever smelled chicken manure, you know it smells worse than any other kind."

The old lady who lived down the hall opened her door and peered out.

"Such talk!" she said, scandalized. "I have a mind to wash out your mouth with soap." She shut the door, probably waiting behind it to hear if he'd call Sproggy any more names. He thought she probably would wash out his mouth. If she could catch him.

Without a word Sproggy turned and pushed the elevator button. Adam let himself into his apartment. He felt ashamed of himself. He shouldn't have said that to her.

"Is that you, Adam?" his mother called. "I'm about

ready." Without answering, he opened the door and peered out cautiously. If Sproggy was still there, he'd say he was sorry.

It was too late. The hall was empty.

CHAPTER 10

"Sorry I ran off at the mouth yesterday," Charlie told Adam next morning. "It's none of my business. But you never heard of sex equality? Women's lib? You don't go around keeping the ladies out of things, clubs, any more. That's old hat. Can't you open up your heart to the little stranger? Just a crack?" Charlie said. "A nice, clean-cut kid like you doesn't have to go around being rude. I think a demon got hold of you, made you talk that way to Sproggy. But now that demon's kaput, right?"

He and Adam shook hands. Adam thought he should've known Charlie wasn't the kind of guy who stayed sore. People who stayed sore a long time weren't as nice as those who made up with no hard feelings. It was something to remember, he told himself. He was glad to be friends with Charlie again. He wasn't sure about the demon, though. He himself had a tendency to stay mad. He'd better get to work on that.

"Me and my wife Millie are signing up for our night courses," Charlie said. "I'm taking art history, modern literature"—he ticked off on his fingers—"and French. When I get so's I can parlez-vous like a native, I'm taking Millie out to a fancy French restaurant and ordering from that menu like I been doing it all my life. Now Millie, she's taking math—she's the checkbook balancer in our house—and playwriting. If you hit it right, there's a lot of money in playwriting, Millie says. We start school next week."

Adam sat down on the steps and watched while Charlie swooshed his mop around.

"I just finished a very interesting story in a magazine," he told Charlie. "About some kids who dug up a mess of gold coins worth a fortune, maybe. Those dumb kids took the stuff to the authorities, and they said the coins might be old pirates' loot. Think of that. Pirates' loot."

Charlie's face grew still the way it did when he listened hard. He pushed his mop around slower and slower until it and he came to a standstill.

"Then you know what happened?" Adam said.

Charlie shook his head, waiting.

"They told them the gold was so old it must've been buried hundreds of years ago, and therefore"—Adam paused dramatically—"therefore the whole lot belonged to the state. Probably if they'd been new coins they would have said they belonged to the city or something. You can't win. You absolutely can't win. Those guys could be instant millionaires, and they don't even get one lousy gold coin as a souvenir. I understand they got a letter from the police chief complimenting them on their honesty. Boy, if it'd been me, I would've sued."

Charlie thought a minute. "If it'd been me," he said dreamily, "I woulda taken the money and run. To the South Seas. Me and Millie always wanted to go to the islands, go snorkeling, eat some flying fish, wear a couple of grass skirts, all like that. In my next life, or if I should by chance win the lottery, that's what me and Millie are going to do. Lie in the sun, take a little nourishment, rest our bones."

"Sounds boring," Adam said.

"Wait'll you're my age, you won't think so," Charlie said. "You get a different perspective on life as you approach your sunset years. Not that I'm getting close, you understand," he added hastily. "I got a few good years left. Actually, I'm in my prime right now."

"What's your prime?" Adam asked.

After a moment's consideration Charlie said, "It's

whatever age you happen to be at the moment. You're in your prime; me and Millie, we're in ours and expect to remain there for many years to come. Once you pass thirty," he said, "you realize you're not immortal." Charlie started to push his mop around again. "The longer you live," he told Adam, "the more you realize that the bread you cast upon the waters comes home to roost. If you get my meaning. If you're nice to your step-sis now when she needs it, someday she'll do you a good turn. One good turn deserves another. And you'll feel good inside, Adam. That's important. You got to treat each day like it was your last. You wake up in the morning with all your buttons, your heart still going, able to put one foot in front of the other, count your blessings. You're able to do a good deed, enjoy life, you're still among the living, you're ahead of the game. That's my philosophy."

"My philosophy is," Adam began, not sure of what he was going to say next, "my philosophy is. . ."

He stared intently at a point just over Charlie's head, trying to look as if his brain were working overtime, as if he were thinking deep thoughts. He had perfected this last year while in fifth grade. He felt it did a great deal to stop his teacher from calling on him to recite because she didn't want to interrupt a great mind at work. But his teacher had been around awhile. She was no dummy. Sometimes she let him get away with his act, sometimes not.

"I haven't got all day," Charlie said. "What's your philosophy?"

"It's that . . . my philosophy is," Adam said, gaining speed, sure now of what he was going to say, "that kindness counts. I think I might become an humanitarian."

"Sounds good," Charlie said. "What is it?"

"A person who does good in the world," Adam explained. "A guy who runs around improving the welfare and happiness of mankind. I looked it up in the dictionary. There was a story in the paper last week about a kid who delivered groceries to an old feeble lady in a third-floor walk-up, and she never even gave him a tip. But he kept delivering and being nice to her. Then she died and left him a bundle. A bunch of dough. Because he was kind to her, she said in a note. How do you like that?"

"Sounds like bread cast upon the waters to me," Charlie said.

"But I wouldn't forget my old friends," he told Charlie. "No matter how important I became, how many times my picture was on TV, I'd remember all my old buddies. You and Kenny and Steve Skully. And even Sproggy." He smiled at Charlie, who looked dubious.

"Listen, kid, I wish you nothing but good luck," Charlie said. "Whatever field you choose, I'll tell folks I knew you when. And it gladdens my heart to hear you include Sproggy in your list of never-to-be-forgotten old buddies. You're a good man, Adam. However, the time has come when the super is going to come around checking on me, and I better say farewell and buckle down."

Adam sat wrapped in a glow of well-being.

"You'll never guess what happened," Sproggy said, bursting into the lobby. "We've decided what kind of club to have. Kenny and I and Steve decided, and I came to let you know."

The glow began to fade, gently, gradually, but fade.

"You're in the club now?" Adam said.

"Oh, yes." Sproggy smiled. "They told me I might join if I paid my dues."

"What kind of club did you decide to have?" Adam said after a minute.

"A chess club," Sproggy announced.

"That lets me out." Adam's glow had gone completely. "I can't play chess."

"Oh, none of us is really good at it," she said. "But we can learn. It's really great fun."

Adam stood up. "I've got stuff to do," he said. "There's just one thing. How much dues did Kenny charge you?"

"It's really very reasonable, I think," Sproggy said. "He said I might join and the dues would be a quarter a week."

Adam put his hands in his pockets and walked in slow motion to the street and toward the river where he could watch the boats fight their way upstream against insuperable odds.

CHAPTER 11

I don't care, Adam thought. He'd lain awake a long time last night telling himself that. I don't care if they made it into a chess club without even asking me. I don't care if they took in a girl. And I don't even care if the girl is Sproggy. He waited for the traffic light to change. Even if they did take her to the cleaner's and charge her a quarter dues. A quarter for joining a stupid dumb club like that one.

He kicked out furiously at a tree. The numbing pain in his big toe made him fiercely glad. Maybe he'd broken his toe. He'd have to have a big cast on it and wouldn't be able to put on his shoe over the cast and might not even have to go to school next week. The trouble with that was that he was looking forward to the opening of school. The first few days were always exhilarating, seeing old friends, getting used to a new teacher, a new classroom. If only school could always be like the opening days, everything would be fine.

Adam stopped at a produce store with a large display of fruits out on the sidewalk.

"I'm looking for some old grapes," he told the owner. "For a parrot."

"You came to the right place," the man said. His eyes were so tiny that Adam didn't think he could see very much out of them. Apparently he could. He took Adam to the back of the store. "Just what you're looking for," he said.

"They look very old to me," Adam said, examining the lot. Even for Burton they looked very beat-up.

"I guarantee their age," the man said. "I'm practically giving them away. They're a real steal."

Adam sniffed and made a face. "You're sure they won't poison anyone?" he said. He wouldn't have minded poisoning Burton in the least, but it occurred to him that Mr. Early might.

"Poison? What's poison?" the man said, wringing his hands at the mere suggestion that he might sell poisoned goods. "You think I could stay in business at the same location twenty-three going on twenty-four years if I sold poisoned goods? Think again. They're a little tired is all. You expect perfection at those prices?''

He had a point. Adam bought the grapes. Using the key Mr. Early had given him, he let himself into the empty apartment. Like a seasoned cat burglar, he tiptoed into the kitchen. The refrigerator was first on his list. Mr. Early was a light eater. Nothing inside but a wizened apple and a lemon with part of its skin gone.

"Oh, no! Not that kid again!" Burton hollered as Adam tiptoed through the living room. That blasted bird was a better watch dog than Rosalie by a long shot. Adam thumbed his nose at Burton and continued into the bedroom.

Mr. Early's closet yielded no valuable camera, no binoculars in a leather case, nothing that a fence downtown would take off Adam's hands at a fat price. The bathroom cabinet was another disappointment. No drugs other than aspirin. He was tempted to dissolve an Alka-Seltzer tablet in a glass of water just to see the bubbles but decided against it. He went into the bedroom, lay down on the floor, and peered underneath the bed. No safe-deposit box hidden there. Nothing but a button and a discarded sock.

So much for his brief career as a cat burglar. He was obviously not destined for a profitable life of crime.

"There you are, Burton baby." Adam dished out some of the grapes into the parrot's dish. "Eat up. It's on the house."

Burton stared stonily at the display, his beady black

eyes fixed on Adam. Then he turned on his perch so he was facing the wall, his hunched shoulders heaving with hate.

Whistling, Adam went to the kitchen to fetch water. When he returned, there was a large, untidy pile of grapes on the floor.

"You better watch it, you better behave, Burton, or you won't get anything more to eat from me," Adam warned. "You better be nice."

The bell rang. If that's her, she's not getting in, Adam thought. He had come to the conclusion that wherever he was, Sproggy would run him to earth. *She is not getting in.*

"Open up in the name of the law!" a voice cried. "I have a search warrant!"

Oh, my gosh. I didn't mean anything. I was only pretending. Adam prepared his speech. I didn't take anything. Search me if you want. I'm clean. He looked through the peephole, expecting the boys in blue. It was terrible, having a guilty conscience. Kenny stood there, Steve behind him. Both were grinning.

"What do you want, creepola?" Adam asked, opening up.

"Nothing. Your mother said you were here. We wanted to case the joint. I never saw a parrot out of a pet store," Kenny said. "I always wanted to get a close look at their feet."

"Their feet? What's special about them?"

"He's only got four toes, coming and going," Kenny said. "I read about them in an encyclopedia."

They all peered intently at Burton's feet. It didn't seem to bother him. He cast a look at them over his shoulder so black and fierce that Kenny shivered.

"Man," he said, "I wouldn't want to meet him in an alley on a dark night. Can he talk?"

"When he feels like it," Adam said. "He threw his dinner on the floor. We'd better pick it up."

"You're the one that's making the bread from this job," Steve pointed out. "You pick it up."

Burton turned and regarded Steve and Kenny in a more friendly fashion.

"Hey, Burton," Kenny said, "give us a few words. A few words for the listening audience."

"You pick it up!" Burton shrieked. He was warming up fast. "You pick it up!"

"If I had any Scotch tape, I'd wrap his whole head in it," Adam said.

"I wouldn't try it," Steve cautioned. "He looks like he might bite your hand off."

"And enjoy doing it," Kenny added.

Burton strutted back and forth on his perch. His proud yellow head was magnificent, his feathers shiny, his insolence enormous. He was clearly enjoying himself.

"My father said parrots live to be about a hundred years old," Steve said. "They outlive most people. Just think. If you take real good care of this here bird, he'll be alive and kicking when you and me and Kenny are six feet under. It makes you stop and think, doesn't it?''

"Six feet under," Burton caroled joyously. "Six feet under."

"Speak for yourself," Adam said sourly. "I'm planning on sticking around a lot longer than this moldy character." He wasn't going to mention the club. He figured he'd wait until one of them brought it up.

Kenny studied Burton closely. "I don't know," he said. "This guy looks like he's good for a long time. It must be boring, though, just sitting there. In the long run, I think human beings have a pretty good deal." For one moment Kenny forgot to be pessimistic. "I mean, they get to go places, eat out, watch TV, stuff like that." He ran out of enjoyable things human beings did. "Is there anything to eat in this joint?" he asked.

"Listen," Adam said sternly, "you just don't go into a strange apartment and help yourself to stuff. I'm being paid to parrot-sit, not to raid the refrigerator. Besides, there's nothing there but an apple and a bald lemon."

"How come you know what's there?" Steve asked.

"I have to check on things," Adam said vaguely.

"I sure am hungry, though," Kenny said.

"My mother says you're a bottomless pit," Adam said.

"No kidding? My mother says the same."

The bell rang again. "What is this, Old Home Week?" Adam said. He peered out the peephole at

Sproggy standing there, holding a paper bag.

"We don't want any," he said. "Whatever you're selling, we don't want any."

Kenny shouldered him aside and took a look for himself. "Speak for yourself, bud," he said and opened the door.

"Welcome to our humble abode," he said. "What you got in the sack?"

"Let me help you with that," Steve said, taking the bag from Sproggy's hands. "Something sure smells good."

"I had to queue up in front of the most extraordinary wagon parked right on the street," Sproggy said, directing her remarks toward Kenny and Steve. She ignored Adam and smiled a good deal at the other two.

"They were selling sausage rolls," Sproggy continued. "They smelled delicious so I bought a bagful. I met Adam's mother downstairs, and she told me he was here, so I took a chance you two would be here also."

She sure moved in fast on this bunch, Adam thought angrily. You'd think she'd known these guys as long as I have.

"I have never heard of a sausage roll in my life," Adam said, blood rushing to his cheeks. He was angry at Sproggy, at Steve and Kenny, and, most of all, at himself. He said in a flat tone, full of dislike, "It sounds fairly disgusting."

Kenny's head disappeared inside the bag. "Oxygen,

give me oxygen,'' he moaned from inside, his voice muffled. "The little lady has purchased what appears to be hot dogs. With mustard and relish.''

"I don't want any,'' Adam said, his mouth watering.

Sproggy, Kenny, and Steve sat cross-legged on the floor and ate. Adam stalked around, talking to Burton. "You're a mess,'' he told the parrot. "I ought to be getting two dollars per diem to take care of you. Look at this cage.''

"We'll split his as long as he doesn't want it,'' Steve decided, breaking Adam's hot dog into thirds, handing the smallest piece to Sproggy and eating the biggest. Kenny devoured his so fast no one had a chance to measure it. "You don't know what you're missing,'' he said.

Adam's stomach rumbled, his mouth filled with saliva. Burton didn't help matters by making a sound, low in his throat, that sounded like a chuckle.

Sproggy laid her backpack on the floor and took out her chess set. "I thought we might practice playing today,'' she said. "I say, it's super to be in a club with you all.'' She smiled at Steve and Kenny. "You have no idea what a difference it makes, having you two for friends.''

Steve and Kenny looked embarrassed. They looked at Adam. He looked at the floor.

"It's our pleasure,'' Kenny mumbled, imitating his father. "It's our pleasure.''

"If I had as many freckles as you, I'd do something about it," Adam said suddenly, wanting to wound and seeing, from her expression, that he'd succeeded.

She put her hand to her face as if it hurt, and she stopped smiling, which, after all, was what he'd wanted. Why, then, did he feel so ashamed?

Kenny looked shocked. "That's rotten, Adam, and you know it," he said.

Burton picked that up. "Rotten Adam," he chortled. "Oh, Adam, rotten, rotten Adam!"

"Shut your lousy mouth or I'll strangle you," Adam snarled.

Burton ruffled his feathers, stared at Adam with his bleak black eyes, and messed on the clean paper on the bottom of his cage.

Kenny took one look and fell on the floor, laughing as if he would never stop. He rolled around, clutching his stomach, tears of laughter rinsing his cheeks.

"Oh, oh, oh!" he moaned. "That bird has got your number. Man, has he got your number!"

"What happened?" Sproggy asked, bewildered.

"I and my father are going to spend Saturday together," Adam said suddenly in a most disagreeable voice. He had made it up on the spot, but it was perfectly plausible. "The two of us. We're going to the Museum of Natural History to see the dinosaurs. Then we'll probably go to the World Trade Center and to a steak house for dinner. Then we might go to a concert at night.''

Sproggy had begun setting out the men on the chess board. That infuriated him further. ''And you'd better not horn in,'' he said. ''We don't want you.''

Sproggy tucked the wrapping from her hot dog into the paper bag neatly and carefully and arose from her spot on Mr. Early's rug. ''You chaps may borrow my set for the afternoon if you like,'' she said. ''I shall go along now. Good-bye.'' She nodded to Steve and Kenny, who sat, amazed at the turn of events. ''We can practice some other time.''

At the door she paused. ''You are beastly,'' she said to Adam, with tears in her eyes, her voice trembling. ''You are the most beastly person I have ever known. I used to think you were nice. I tried to like you. Mummy told me I'd like you, and I did. But not now.'' She slung her pack over her shoulder and left.

''Beastly rotten!'' Burton shouted, having the time of his life. ''Beastly rotten!''

The three boys sat still, avoiding one another's eyes. Space grew around Adam, like fungus on a tree stump, separating him from Kenny and Steve. Silence made the room seem hot and stuffy and crowded, as if it were filled with bodies. Adam opened a window to let in some air.

''I guess it's time for this dumb bird's stupid soap

92-

opera," he said. "Can you imagine anything as stupid as a parrot watching *All My Children*?"

Burton settled on his perch like an old lady anticipating her afternoon outing. He gave the screen his rapt attention.

"What'd you do that for?" Kenny asked, his voice high and thin, like a violin playing in the distance. "She's not all that bad."

"Why'd you have to take her in the club?" Adam said. "You didn't even tell me it was a chess club now. I didn't know you guys knew how to play chess, even. How come nobody asked me what I thought?"

"I told you my brother was teaching me how to play," Kenny said, on the defensive. "My father taught him and he's teaching me."

"How about you?" Adam asked Steve.

"I read a book about it," Steve said. "We were going to tell you. We just didn't get around to it."

"Well, I don't play, so that lets me out, right? That lets me out right on my butt. I didn't want to be in that club, anyway."

"That's what you told us. You said you were going to quit." Kenny and Steve got up and dusted crumbs all over the rug.

"If she didn't have a quarter to pay your lousy dues, you wouldn't give her the time of day, and you know it," Adam said deliberately.

"That's not true," Kenny said in a loud voice. "We'd take her in even if she didn't have the bread."

"How about you? You guys pay the twenty-five cents?" Adam asked, smiling at them in an unfriendly fashion.

"We each put an IOU in the till," Steve said. "When we get our allowance, we pay up."

"You guys make me laugh," Adam said. He felt like bawling. "You really make me laugh."

Kenny opened his mouth, closed it. At the door he turned. "There's nothing wrong with Sproggy," he said. "She's an O.K. kid. I and Steve like her. We like her a lot. Come on," he said to Steve. "Let's split."

Adam and Burton were alone. Crouched in front of the TV, they watched, waiting for the unraveling of terrible events, the inevitable disasters, listening to the droning voices, the sad music, while outside the sun shone.

And inside, all was sadness and woe.

CHAPTER 12

The sound of rain on the windows, which woke Adam Thursday morning, suited his mood. It would probably rain every day until Monday, the first day of school. On Monday the sun would shine in a cloudless sky.

"Ma," he said at breakfast, dallying with his egg, waiting for the precise right moment to prick the yolk and watch it ooze over his plate. When he was little, his mother had recited a verse to him which went:

> *Oh, what a fork prick,*
> *Oh, what a thrust.*
> *My beautiful yellow middle*
> *Is bust.*

It was his favorite poem.

"Ma, how come I got no ethnic background?" he said.

She stopped reading the paper long enough to look at him over the top of her glasses.

"How come you ain't got no ability to speak properly, either?" she asked.

"I mean it. I got no ethnic background," he complained. "Everybody else I know has got one. Charlie's got blood from all over. His wife Millie, too. Mr. Early told me he came to Ellis Island from Austria when he was two years old. And Kenny said his great-great-grandfather was a horse thief in the old country and escaped to America by changing his name. Of course"— Adam broke his toast into tiny pieces—"with Kenny, you got to take everything with a grain of salt. But me. I got nothing to brag about except I was born in Brooklyn. Big deal."

"You are some deprived kid," his mother said. "My heart bleeds for you. Your ethnic background is as good as anyone else's."

"I bet even that creep Sproggy has an ethnic background." Adam went on complaining, not hearing what his mother said. "I wouldn't be surprised to hear she had a couple of ancestors who fought dragons and slew them. I wouldn't mind slewing some myself."

"Slaying," she said.

"What?"

"Never mind." She shrugged. "I have the feeling I'm fighting a losing battle. But you really are being petty about that child. There's nothing wrong with her. She's rather nice. And very bright. And your father doesn't love you less because Sproggy is his stepdaughter."

"Who said he did?" Adam said rudely. His mother raised her eyebrows at him.

"What's my ethnic background, then, if it's so hot?" he asked in a belligerent tone. He was tired of talking about Sproggy, thinking about her, worrying about her. In a few days she had charged into his life uninvited and upset more than one applecart. Next thing she'd be president of the club, ordering Steve and Kenny about as if she really *was* a Mafioso.

"Well . . ." His mother stopped to think. "My grandmother was Italian and my grandfather Irish. How's that for starters? And your father's paternal grandparents were White Russians."

"Cool," said Adam. "How about a black Russian? Do I have any of those?"

"Not that I know of. You want everything, don't you?" She got up to get another cup of coffee. Adam licked the last vestiges of egg from his plate. He loved to do this, especially after eating pancakes. The maple syrup tasted better that way than straight out of the bottle.

"Stop that!" she called from the kitchen.

How did she always know? Once, years ago when he was practically still in diapers, she'd told him she had eyes in the back of her head. For a while he'd believed her, even though, no matter how hard he looked, lifting up her hair and searching under it, he never could find those eyes.

"I have to go feed Burton," Adam said after he'd cleared the table. "And I might go down to talk to Charlie. He signed up to take courses in night school yesterday. Him and his wife Millie are both going back to school. Charlie says education is the key. He says he might be a big shot someday."

A few minutes later his mother held up the newspaper. "Look at this. Just cast your eye on this." There on page three, big as life, dressed in a shirt and tie and jacket, was Charlie, smiling as if his face might split in two.

The write-up under the picture read:

DROPOUT AT 13, HANDYMAN NAMED LEADER
OF SPECIAL CONTINUING EDUCATION WEEK

Special Continuing Education Week, so designated by the Mayor, will honor a group of visiting European and American college presidents, as well as one enrollee, selected at random to represent the new breed of student who is taking advantage of the city's expanding educational opportunities. Charles Hagelstrom, handyman in an East Side apartment building, left school in the eighth grade and has been named Special Continuing Student of the Week. He and his wife Millie have enrolled in City University night classes. "I admire education," Hagelstrom says. "I admire an educated man. Education is the key to better living, and I hope to better myself and the world around me when my wife and I take a variety of courses at the night school."

Adam snatched the paper from his mother's hand. "Bring it right back, Mom," he shouted. When he reached the lobby, two other tenants were shaking Charlie's hand, exclaiming over what a fine likeness the picture was.

"Would have known you anywhere," an old lady was saying. "Doesn't do you justice, though. You're much younger looking in the flesh." The thin man with her agreed.

Charlie beamed. "That's what my wife Millie says," he said. "I wanted her to get in the picture, too, but she said no. She's shy, my wife Millie is. When she gets to know you, she's not, but first meeting, she backs off."

"I'll save you my copy," the old lady said.

"Thanks, I'd appreciate that," Charlie said. The super, Mr. Courtney, came out of the back room and scowled. "Work to be done, Charlie," he said. "You'll have to be a celebrity on your own time." He smiled, revealing a set of perfectly matched yellow teeth, to show he was only joking.

They took the hint and cleared out. "Hey, Charlie," Adam said, waving the paper in his face. "Next thing you know, people will be stopping you on the street, asking for your autograph."

Mr. Courtney stood there, waiting.

"See you around, Adam," Charlie said. "I'll only give it to 'em on a blank check made out to me."

If I took Burton out for a walk, Adam thought, he might drown in a puddle. He'd never seen a parrot on the end of a leash, but that didn't mean there couldn't be a first time. He could see the headlines now: PARROT DROWNS IN PUDDLE. BOY MAKES VALIANT RESCUE ATTEMPT. MENTIONED FOR MEDAL.

"I say, Charlie!" Sproggy burst into the lobby, enveloped in a streaming slicker. She looked around, at and through Adam.

"Charlie, are you there?" she called.

The super appeared. "Our local big shot has work to do," he said sarcastically. "Just leave your calling card and I'll have him call you."

"I'll come back later," she said and went back out into the rain.

I'm invisible, the invisible Bionic Man, Adam decided. A spell has been cast upon me. I'm fated to spend the rest of my days haunting empty rooms.

He opened the door to see how far Sproggy had got. There she was, standing on the corner. I'm sorry, he moved his mouth to say. I'm sorry I was mean. But although his lips moved, no words came out.

CHAPTER 13

Adam let himself into Mr. Early's apartment as soundlessly as a wisp of a British pea souper. Just once, he thought, just once I want to sneak up on that bird. Thinks he's so smart. Thinks he's king of the birds.

He peeked into the living room. Great mounds of discarded seeds and fruit were scattered in an untidy circle around Burton's cage. Boy and bird stared stonily at each other.

"I say!" Burton shrieked. "Oh, I say, not that kid again!" He strutted back and forth on his perch, his great yellow head proud and handsome, his large black eyes filled with fierce glee.

Adam spread clean paper on the bottom of the cage and waited. The paper remained clean. Maybe Burton was constipated. That was *his* problem.

One foot out the door, Adam paused.

"Go soak your head!" he shouted and slammed the door before Burton could answer back. It was the little victories in life that counted, Adam decided, set up by this littlest victory of all.

Killing time, he walked in slow motion down the stairs to his own apartment. "Guess I'll take Rosie for a walk," he told his mother, who was washing her brushes at the sink.

"I got exactly the right expression on my faces this morning," she said dreamily. "Exactly right. Maybe I'll take the afternoon off. It's raining," she said.

"That's Rosie's kind of weather. It makes her hair curly," Adam replied, snapping the leash to Rosie's collar.

The river was gray and rough, the park deserted. A large poodle, whom Rosalie had tangled with on occasion, pranced about, escorted by a gentleman in a leisure suit decorated with nailheads. Rosalie moved in closer to Adam, so close he tripped on her.

"Act your age," he told her in a low, severe tone. That poodle was thirty miles of bad road, acting as if he owned the city, sniffing at every tree, lifting his feet high like a horse in Madison Square Garden. Who did he think he was?

Twin corgis on identical pale blue leashes, led by a lady with night-black hair and fingernails so long and red and sharp they could have doubled as butchers' knives, barked frantically at Rosalie. She went limp. Like so many others, she was not her best in a crisis. She wasn't known as the Terror of Eighty-eighth Street for nothing, Adam knew.

"Listen," he whispered in disgust, "if you let two little wimps like them scare you, you've had it."

Rosalie pulled herself together and lunged at the corgis, secure in the knowledge that Adam held the other end of her leash. If he ever let go and left her free to attack, Adam knew she probably would die of fright right on the sidewalk. As it was, the corgis retreated, rolling their eyes back in their heads in panic. Adam smiled at the lady, who gave him a look of loathing.

"Come, girls," she said, curling the edges of her mouth in a silly way. "It's time for your rest." That's the kind of dogs they were. They took rests.

The black-haired lady looked at Rosalie.

"What breed is that?" she asked, haughty as a princess.

"She's very rare," Adam said truthfully. The lady drew her sweater around her, put a scarf on her head so her hair wouldn't run, and pulled her twins homeward.

Adam waited until she'd got some distance away. Then he called out, "You better curb those little finks or

I'll report them to the cops!'' and dove around the corner of the building so she couldn't chase him.

It began to rain hard. Adam decided to seek shelter in the pizza parlor down the street. He might run into someone he knew with a slice nobody had room for.

Two men were sitting at the end of the counter, arguing quietly. The bigger one poked the other in the chest several times, saying, ''You get my meaning?''

Sproggy sat at the counter, surrounded on one side by Janice the Grub and on the other by Freddy the Freeloader. Both were famous for being around when someone else was paying for the eats.

''I'm so glad you could come with me,'' Sproggy said. ''What kind of pizza do you want?''

Janice didn't even have to check the menu. She knew it by heart.

''I'll have the pepperoni,'' she said. ''And put extra cheese on it.''

''The same,'' Freddy said.

Sproggy nodded. ''That'll be fine,'' she said. ''Is one pizza enough for all of us?'' she asked the man behind the counter.

''Depends,'' he said. ''You want it to go?''

''To go where?'' Sproggy asked.

''He means you want to eat it here or take it out,'' Janice explained. ''You're only getting one? For all of us?''

"It's all I have money for," Sproggy said.

"I don't know," Janice the Grub said. "I'm pretty hungry."

"Do you have any money?" Sproggy asked. "We could order another if you do."

"No, that's O.K.," Janice said hastily.

Adam laughed silently to himself when he heard that. He reckoned that on her tombstone they'd put: Here lies Janice the Grub who wouldn't turn down a free deck chair on the *Titanic*.

He caught a glimpse of Sproggy's face as she turned on the stool, and he felt a surge of something so subtle, so unfamiliar, that at first he didn't know it for what it was: sympathy.

Sympathy, raising its head, waving to him, striving to be recognized.

Adam sneered at himself for a couple of minutes, trying to catch a glimpse of his image in the dirty window glass. Nothing he could do would make any difference. Sproggy was being taken by a couple of first-class creeps who'd run out of other people to take. She must really be hard up for friends, he thought. And that was partly his fault. Maybe if he walked up to the counter and slapped her on the back and said something nice, it would help. She'd probably spit on him.

Freddy was busy loading his pockets with sugar cubes. Neither one of them had paid for a pizza or a stick of gum within living memory. They were famous for grubbing: other people's sandwiches, notebooks, anything. Last year Janice had even grubbed Kenny's new tan sweater, but his mother called her mother and they got it back.

Adam hung around by the door, listening. "Shut that door, there's a draft!" the little guy at the counter shouted in a loud, deep voice. So Adam went out again into the rain and wondered if he should clue Sproggy in on her companions. Never mind. It wouldn't do any good. She wouldn't listen. His feelings of sympathy faded. Let her find out for herself. He hung around in the doorway of the jewelry store, waiting for them to come out.

"No loitering!" the owner shouted from behind locked doors. To freak him out, Adam said, "I just wanted to price the watch in the window."

The owner said, "Sorry, sir," sliding back about eighteen locks and sticking his head out. "Fifty-five dollars, with a year's guarantee."

"I was thinking more of something in the hundred-dollar range," Adam said. The man shouted a couple of insults at Adam and relocked his door. Adam peered into the window of the pizza parlor. There they were, at the counter, jaws moving rhythmically, staring straight ahead, while Sproggy chattered away happily, enjoying herself with her friends.

If she only knew, Adam thought. For lack of anything better to do, he dropped Rosalie off at the apartment and went upstairs to check on Burton. He liked being alone in Mr. Early's apartment. He pretended it was his own.

Mr. Early was lying on the sofa, covered with a knitted blanket.

"Got home early," he said in a faint voice. "Must've eaten something that didn't agree with me. My sister had a party last night, served a punch with strawberries floating in it. Should have known. Anything with strawberries floating in it has got to be poison to my system."

"You want me to get anything for you?" Adam said, sitting down.

Mr. Early shook his head. "See you took care of Burton real well," he said. "Good boy. My sister was trying to fix me up with one of her widow friends. They're the ones who like the strawberry stuff. One of those ladies, she's pretty well fixed, I guess. Winters in Florida and has a nice little place on the Jersey shore for summers. You ever been to the Jersey shore?"

Adam shook his head. He had discovered the best approach with Mr. Early was to keep quiet and listen.

"I wouldn't dare set my foot in the water down there," Mr. Early said. "Those waves'd knock you down as soon as they'd look at you. By and large, women talk too much. I enjoy my solitude. My Ida knew how to be quiet. Burton and I are company for each other. That sand gets in your bathing suit something fierce when you go in the ocean down in Jersey.

Fills it up so you can't hardly move. And cold. Lands, but it's cold. You two get on all right?''

"Sure," Adam said, avoiding Burton's malevolent, hooded eyes. Burton, for once, said nothing.

Mr. Early raised himself on his elbows. "I'm going to pay you the full amount I owe," he said. "Not your fault I came back early." He counted out three one-dollar bills and added a dime.

"There's a tip for you," he said. "A job well done."

"I can't take all that," Adam protested. "I didn't do that much. Just give me a buck and we'll call it even."

Mr. Early lay back, shaking his head. "That widow lady I was telling you about, she's a vegetarian. Says it keeps her young, not eating meat. That and using honey in her tea instead of sugar. What I say is"—he sat up again—"what good's it do to stay young if you can't have your innards when you want 'em? I could never care for a lady who's a vegetarian. Otherwise, she's real nice. Sort of reminded me of Ida."

He sighed deeply. "I could use a glass of milk," he said. "Nice cold milk. Will you run around the corner and get me a quart?"

When Adam got back from the store, Charlie was waiting in the lobby.

"You'll never guess what happened," Charlie said. "Never in a million years."

"You won the lottery?" Adam said.

"No, but almost as good. Sit down while I tell you because I don't want you to hurt yourself when you fall down." Charlie pushed Adam into the lobby's solitary gray chair.

"Me and Millie are going to Gracie Mansion," Charlie said slowly, spacing each word for the fullest effect. "We been invited to go to a party on Sunday at the Mayor's place. On account of my picture in the paper, going to City University and all. They're having a reception for a bunch of bigwigs—educators, college presidents, all like that—and me and Millie are included due to the fact that we're representative of the type of folks going back to school in this great city of ours. Now what have you got to say? Eh?"

Adam was struck dumb with astonishment.

"I didn't tell her yet," Charlie went on. "One of the Mayor's aides, he called up here a few minutes ago. I thought it was somebody pulling my leg. But he said it was for real, and I believe him. He said the invitation would come in the mail tomorrow. I want to see Millie's face when I tell her. The super says I can go home early, as soon as I finish washing down the walls in the back hall."

"I'll give you a hand," Adam said.

"That's a real friendly thing to do," Charlie said. "I'm almost done, though. You're a pal, Adam, a real pal."

"Congratulations." Adam shook Charlie's hand.

"You've made the big time. Only celebrities get invited to the Mayor's pad. Maybe you'll be on TV. I wouldn't be surprised. You better plan a speech, Charlie. They might ask you to give a speech."

"Never!" Charlie wiped his brow, perspiring at the mere thought of giving a speech at Gracie Mansion. "I couldn't do that, Adam. I never gave a speech in my entire life. I'm too old to start now."

"Since when are you too old to do something?" Adam scowled at Charlie. "Since when? I thought you said you were in your prime. You and Millie both. Isn't that what you said?"

"Right, right," Charlie agreed, although he still looked nervous. "I'll see you around, kid," he said.

Adam took the milk up to Mr. Early and told him of Charlie's good fortune.

"I call that super, as your little stepsister would say," Mr. Early said. "Absolutely top hole!"

"Top hole!" Burton shouted from the next room.

"It's time for *All My Children*," Mr. Early said, looking at his watch. "You want to stay and watch with Burton and me?"

"No thanks," Adam said. "I got problems enough of my own."

"That's just it," Mr. Early said, turning on the TV. "Nothing you got bothering you can be as bad as these folks."

"That's what you think," Adam said.

CHAPTER 14

Adam dreamed that night of becoming the tallest man in the world. His legs began to stretch in a most delightful fashion. At first it was marvelous. He roamed the streets, looking down on all the little folk, not to mention peering into the Empire State Building and the World Trade Center and, stooping, the Central Park zoo. For openers.

He'd waited a long time for this.

Offers to play basketball flooded in. His mother was kept busy handling his phone calls while he was out on the street, letting people look at him in amazement, touch him, ask for his autograph.

Once started, however, his legs wouldn't quit. His body stayed the same size. It seemed as if his head would touch the sky. His picture was on the front page of the paper, and, naturally, he was on TV, answering dumb questions. He had to bend down to talk into the microphone. It was interesting to see the respect with which he was treated. Surely he, too, would be bidden to attend a party at Gracie Mansion.

None of his friends were allowed to play with him any more. Their mothers were afraid he might crush them by mistake.

After the novelty wore off, doctors were called in to see if they could stop the growing process. He was given massive doses of anti-vitamins. Fortune tellers who promised they could help—NO MATTER WHAT YOUR PROBLEM IS: GUARANTEED RESULTS—were consulted.

Nothing did any good.

His mother, her temper frayed, said, "I can't sit here day after day answering those dopey phone calls. I've got work to do."

Abruptly the scene shifted, and he and Sproggy were standing in line at a hot-dog wagon. He was first, and although he had no money, the man handed him a bag bursting with food. Behind him, Sproggy thrust out her hand, full of money. But the man, who had suddenly become Janice the Grub, grabbed it and then handed Sproggy an empty bag. Adam ran away, and Sproggy, looking like the little match girl, pursued him, weeping. Then Janice began to chase them both and, fortunately, he woke up.

Throwing back the covers, he thought, I will be nice to her. I will practice being an humanitarian. He checked and breathed a sigh of relief. He was the same size he'd been yesterday. It was a delicious feeling. For once, he was satisfied. He put on his clothes, brushed his teeth, and, in a rush of well-being, made his bed.

"Kenny called," his mother said while they had breakfast. "I wish you'd tell him not to call so early. He woke me up. He said there's a club meeting scheduled for this afternoon. Second bench along the river, as usual. And don't forget to bring your dues, he said."

"I told him I wasn't going to be in his stupid old club," Adam said. "If she's in, I'm out."

"By 'she' I suppose you mean Sproggy?"

"You know something, Mom? I never told you this, but that night that I and Dad went out to dinner he asked me to look out for her. For Sproggy. He said Arabella was worried about her and I should take care of her." Adam laughed a hollow, mirthless laugh. "That's a big fat laugh. She can take care of herself. And a slew of other guys too."

"Did you tell Dad you would look out for her?" his mother asked.

"Yes," Adam said. "I promised I would. That was before I knew her. Really knew her, I mean. There's a

114-

lot of stuff I could tell you," he said darkly to his mother, "but I don't want you to worry."

"If you promised, I guess you'd better follow through as best you can." She buttered a piece of toast. "One thing about your father, if he promises something, only a catastrophe would stop him from keeping that promise. And he expects the same from you."

Adam sighed. "I was afraid of that," he said. "If you only knew, Mom, what I'm going through."

"I wish you'd talk to me about what's bothering you, Adam," she said. "That's what mothers are for. It might make you feel better if we talked about it. I'll listen, you know that."

"Who do you talk to when things bother you?" Adam asked her. "You never tell me when you're worried."

"Sometimes I do," she said.

"Did you used to talk to Dad about stuff?" he said. "When you were married?"

"Always," she said. "Well, not always but most times."

"Ma, I was wondering about something," Adam said. He'd been thinking about this for a while, and now seemed the time to ask.

"Yes?"

"That night that Dad was here, with Harry and me," he said.

"Yes?" His mother had become completely still.

She looked at him, giving him her full attention.

"Well, I was just wondering how it was to see Dad again, after he got married to Arabella. And everything," he finished lamely.

"I felt a little sad, I guess," she said after some thought. "I'll always have a special feeling for your father. He was my first love, really. I think I'll always love him just a little, but I'm happier not being married to him. Do you understand?"

"Not really," Adam said. But he was relieved at her answer. He'd been afraid she might be unhappy because his father was married to someone else. "Do you think he thinks she's as pretty as you are?" he said.

"Not likely," she said in an English accent, and they both laughed. It was all right.

"I might tell you in a little while what's on my mind," Adam said. "It's getting better, though," he sighed. "There are just some things you can't tell your mother right away," he said.

"Good heavens, that sounds ominous." She brushed his hair off his forehead. "It can't be that bad. Can it?"

"It depends on what you mean by 'that bad,' " Adam said. "What's bad to you isn't necessarily bad to me. And vice versa."

She thought about that for a minute. "That's true," she said. "You are getting older and wiser, my friend."

"I know," he said.

For lack of anything better to do, he cruised by the park bench to see what was going on. Nothing. Low clouds scudded in the sky, and the sunlight filtered through without much enthusiasm. A couple of guys were throwing a Frisbee around. Adam stood and watched. They didn't throw it his way or even look at him, so he moved on.

"Hey," he said to the guard at Gracie Mansion, "a friend of mine's coming to a party here on Sunday."

"Sunday's my day off," the guard said. "I and the wife are going to New Rochelle for her folks' wedding anniversary. Thirty-five glorious years of togetherness. We all chipped in and bought them a color TV. They'll cry when they see it."

Adam nodded. A jogger came down East End Avenue, head back, mouth open, eyes half shut. Joggers always looked as if they were in agony, Adam thought, but they must be having a good time. Otherwise, why would they jog? Life was full of questions and very few answers, Adam decided.

When he checked a little later, Steve and Kenny were sitting there, waiting.

"It's about time," Steve said.

"I wasn't sure I was coming," Adam said, "after the fight. I told you guys I wasn't in the club any more. Where's Sproggy? Trying to scare up another quarter?"

"You're a million laughs," Kenny told him.

"She couldn't come today. We wanted to have a

business meeting, settle our finances," Steve said. "My father says if an organization's finances are in a muddle, it's in trouble."

"Why don't we ask your father to join?" Adam asked sarcastically.

"Oh, he's too busy." Steve was serious.

"I'm the treasurer, right?" Kenny said. "I'm in charge of collecting the dues." He checked his notebook. "You're in arrears," he told Adam.

"I told you I was out," Adam said. "If it's a chess club, I can't play chess so that lets me out."

"We changed it," Steve said. "We're going to make it an investment club instead. We study the market, read the report every day, and plan on what stocks we'll invest in."

Kenny saw Adam looking at him. "That was his idea," he said, pointing to Steve. "Not mine."

"Why'd you change it from a chess club?" Adam asked.

"It was Sproggy," Kenny said with a long face. "She beat us all the time. She kept stealing our pawns. It wasn't any fun, her winning all the time, so we decided to change."

Adam was glad. He couldn't help himself. "Is she going to be in the investment club?" he said. She'll corner the market, he thought. He didn't know what cornering the market meant, except that it was good, but it seemed logical that Sproggy would accomplish this feat.

"Sure," Steve said, "she paid her dues."

"Yeah, I heard," Adam said. "What about not letting in girls? I thought that's what we decided."

"She's not like a regular girl," Kenny said. "I mean, she doesn't giggle and she doesn't give us a hard time. Not like my sisters."

"If she was your sister, she'd give you a hard time," Adam told him.

"You got a point," Kenny agreed. "But she's sort of your sister and she doesn't give you a hard time."

Adam shrugged. No sense going into that. Sproggy was taller, stronger, smarter, able to handle herself better than he was.

And he had to learn to live with that· and follow through on the promise he'd made to his father.

He couldn't do it. It was too tough, looking after a red-headed Mafioso. Maybe if he was eleven he could handle her. But ten, as he'd already found out, was a bad age.

It wasn't until he was almost home that he realized he'd forgotten to tell Steve and Kenny about Charlie going to a party at Gracie Mansion. He'd call first thing in the morning.

CHAPTER 15

Adam slept late Saturday. When he woke, it was already six. He got a glass of orange juice and turned on the TV. A program about agriculture in the U.S.A. was the best bet. Then he had to make a choice between *Sunrise Semester* and *Casper and Friends*. He settled on *Casper*. Rosalie watched for a couple of minutes, but ghosts always freaked her out so she disappeared.

The sun might come out today. Two days left until school. Adam stood on his head for a while. The TV wasn't any better or worse that way. Just different. The orange juice threatened to come back up so he lay flat on the floor, staring at the ceiling.

Tomorrow was the big one. He couldn't wait to station himself at the fence outside Gracie Mansion and watch Charlie go up the steps, an honored and invited guest. If it couldn't be him, he was glad it was Charlie. Second place was better than none. He'd get all the scoop from Charlie and have plenty to tell his friends. With what Charlie said and his own vivid imagination, he could get together a pretty good story. Fact and fiction were not inseparable, Adam had long ago discovered.

"How come you slept so late?" he asked his mother as she wandered out to the kitchen, yawning.

She only looked at him. She didn't like to talk much when she first woke up.

"I've been up for hours," Adam said. "I'm going to goof off today," he told her. "Not do much of anything."

She drank her first cup of coffee.

"That'll be a nice change," she said when she'd finished.

The telephone rang. It was Mr. Early. "Hope I didn't wake you," he said.

"That's O.K.," Adam told him. "I've been up for hours."

"Me, too. The thing is, I'm going down to Jersey again, if you can believe it." Mr. Early laughed apologetically. "That widow I told you about? Well, she called last night, asked me down for Sunday dinner.

Says she's got a special dish she worked up just for me. Liver and sausage rolls wrapped in bacon. Sounds mighty tasty, eh?"

Adam made a noise which could've meant almost anything. He thought of saying that Sproggy called hot dogs sausage rolls but decided against it. It seemed he and Mr. Early always wound up talking about food, disgusting food.

"She says the ocean's been like a bathtub," Mr. Early went on, "so I told her I'd take the bus down. God knows I can't stand much of that ocean, even if it is like a bathtub. Fills my suit up with sand, like I told you, so I can hardly stand up."

The idea of Mr. Early in a bathing suit boggled Adam's mind.

"Will you feed Burton again for me? I'll be home on the first bus Monday morning, so if you'll pop in on Sunday I'd appreciate it," Mr. Early said. "I know you have a very important engagement Monday morning so you want to get your rest Sunday night. I can hear those old school bells ringing right this minute." He laughed. "Can you manage Burton on Sunday?"

"Sure," Adam said.

"Same rates," Mr. Early said.

"You don't have to pay me. You already overpaid," Adam said.

"It's worth it to me. You're a reliable, trustworthy

worker," Mr. Early said. "Not too many like you around these days."

After he'd hung up, Adam thought about that. I don't know, he said to himself. I know a bunch of reliable, trustworthy kids. There's Kenny. Well, maybe. Not as good as me, I don't think. There's Steve. So-so. How about a girl in his class named Emily MacFadden? She was both those things. She got to take messages to the principal's office, collect papers, cleaned the blackboard, everything. Emily was prim and well-behaved. Her neck was always clean. When she wrote a book report, you could tell she'd read every word, not just the first and last chapter and the front flap, like some he could mention.

Adam headed for the river. There was something soothing about watching the water move, he thought. Maybe he'd be a tugboat captain when he grew up.

As Adam rounded the corner of Eighty-eighth Street and East End Avenue, the brisk wind caught him in the face, bringing the river smell to his nose. And to his ears came a racket from a group of girls across the street. It looked like Janice the Grub and some of her cronies standing in a circle, chanting at someone or something Adam couldn't see.

"Evangelion!" they shouted, "Evangelion!" and the circle let out a roar that would likely wake the Mayor if he was still asleep. If they weren't careful, Adam thought, the guard would think they were a radical group demonstrating against something and call the police.

A mad flurry of activity inside the circle caused the formation to break slightly. The girls put up their arms to protect themselves from a swinging object that clipped them on their heads. Adam had a sudden feeling that he knew who was landing those blows.

"You stop that, you just stop that!" Janice the Grub shrieked. A girl with a nasty, molelike face shouted, "Pip pip and all that sort of rot, Evangelion!" and started to run away.

He'd been right. It was Sproggy, swinging her backpack, taking off after the fleeing tormentor. Just as she was about to come close enough to land another blow, Sproggy fell. Flat on the sidewalk. Adam had done that. He knew how it felt, how the wind was knocked out of you and the temptation to throw up was intense. The group left behind pulled themselves together, adjusted their clothing, and made no effort to help Sproggy. They stood, pointing at her.

"Serves her right," Adam heard one of them say. "Nasty thing. Why doesn't she go back where she came from? What a stupid name!" They turned and walked away. The girl Sproggy had been chasing was nowhere in sight. Adam figured she was still running.

"You all right, Sproggy?" he said, putting out his

hand to her. Her nose was running, her face wet with tears. She closed her eyes for a minute, shook her head, taking deep breaths. Adam put his hands behind his back and looked away from her, giving her a chance to pull herself together. "If you want, I'll give you a hand up," he said.

She sat up and rubbed her knee. "I shall be quite all right in a moment," she said, "but I don't have a hand-kerchief." She wiped her nose on her sleeve. Adam fumbled in his pockets. He found a necktie he'd stuffed in his pants weeks ago. He handed it to her, and she blew her nose as best she could on the slippery red and yellow striped tie. "Thank you," she said. "I'll ask Mummy to wash it out and return it."

"Oh, that's O.K., I don't need it," Adam replied. "You O.K.?" he asked. He thought, this must be the first time in her life she's ever been trounced. And humiliated.

"I thought she was my friend," Sproggy said, sniffing. "Then she found out my name was Evangeline and she told them and they started to make fun of me. How can I help it if my name's Evangeline? I don't think that's such a bad name, do you?"

Adam considered. "I never heard it before," he said. "I never knew what your name was. I guess it's not so bad, once you get used to it. Anyway, what difference does it make?"

"A great deal," Sproggy said, very dignified.

"I like Sproggy better," Adam said. "Sproggy's a nice name."

Her face brightened. "Do you really think so?" she said. "I'm so glad. Do you know that's the first time you ever said anything nice to me?" she said in astonishment.

Adam had the grace to blush. He felt ashamed. She had spoken the truth.

"Come on, let's get out of here." Adam put out his hand again, and this time she took it and pulled herself upright.

"They didn't know I was such a good shot with my backpack," she said. "I have very good aim."

"Yes," Adam said in a respectful voice, "you do." He promised himself he'd stay out of her way, never aggravate her again.

"It was very kind of you to come to my rescue," Sproggy said. "Thank you, Adam."

He felt himself getting red in the face. It was the first time anyone had called him kind. "You want a Coke?" he said.

"I don't have any money," Sproggy said.

"I meant I'd treat you," Adam told her. "I have some money from Mr. Early for feeding Burton."

"Oh, that would be super!" Sproggy cried. "How simply ripping!" and she slung her backpack into place on her shoulder, narrowly missing Adam's head. They walked over toward the deli on York Avenue.

"Hey, buddy," a large, scroungy young man in blue jeans said to Adam, "got a quarter?"

Adam thought fast. "I was just going to ask you the same thing," he said coolly. "Me and my sister here, we ain't eaten in two days."

"No kidding?" The young man dipped into his pocket. "Hey, I can't stand seeing a couple of kids starve. Be my guest." He handed Adam two quarters. "It's not much, but it's my whole day's take," he said. "Things are slow this time of year."

"Thanks," Adam said.

Sproggy's mouth hung open. She said nothing. Zilch. Adam took long, slow, high steps. The Bionic Man off to the deli. He felt very good. She followed close behind him.

"How super! How absolutely super!" she said.

"I bet you thought that guy was a creep, didn't you?" Adam said. "And he turned out to be a nice guy."

"You told him I was your sister."

"Two ice-cold Cokes, please," Adam said to the clerk.

"To go," said Sproggy.

The clerk looked surprised. "I didn't think you were going to drink them here," he said.

CHAPTER 16

When Adam went up to Mr. Early's Sunday morning, Burton seemed depressed. His feathers drooped, his eyes had lost their luster, and he was unusually quiet. Adam ladled out the seeds and replenished the water.

"Too bad you're missing the party today at the Mayor's house," he said. "Everyone's going. I understand they're serving cheese and crackers and smoked parrot."

Burton's hooded eyes regarded Adam dispassionately.

"Did you hear me?" Adam raised his voice. "I said they're having smoked parrot on the menu. What do you think of that?" Burton said nothing. "You must be

coming down with something. You got a sore throat?''
Adam said.

No response. What fun was that? "I'll tell you how it tasted," Adam said. He went to the door. "I'm going now. You got one more chance to talk. Speak now or forever hold your peace."

Burton opened his mouth and let out a squawk of such magnitude Adam thought it could be heard down on the street. The squawk became a laugh and Burton laughed until Adam was in the elevator. Adam fancied he could still hear it after he'd let himself into his own apartment. He took a shower and put on his new school clothes. The red sweater was his favorite. If he wore his new red sweater, Charlie could spot him outside the fence and might wave. He was looking forward to Charlie's going to this party as much as Charlie was, he imagined.

And Millie. Although he'd never met Charlie's wife Millie, he'd heard so much about her he thought he knew exactly what she looked like. She was a big woman with a warm and merry smile. She wore glasses and polka-dotted dresses. Blue polka dots. She had brown hair and smelled like chocolate chip cookies. She laughed a lot and read bits and pieces out of the newspaper to Charlie during TV commercials. That much Adam knew for a fact. Charlie had told him Millie didn't believe in wasting a minute of the day. And while the TV program was on, Millie knitted or made quilts.

"Millie is a beautiful person," Charlie had told him more than once. Adam knew this must be so.

"Kenny called while you were gone," his mother said. "He'll meet you in the park. At the usual bench, he said. Steve and he have some hot tips they want to talk over with you."

"I'm not talking about financial matters on Sunday," Adam told her. "Sunday is a day of rest. Those guys don't know when to quit. Since when do we have club meetings on Sunday, anyway?"

"You got me," she said. "Come out to the kitchen with me so we can talk. I have a big project going. I promised Harry I'd fix osso buco for him."

"Is that Chinese?" Adam asked.

"Nope, it's veal knuckle," she said.

Veal knuckle? It sounded like something Mr. Early would like. Adam was so grossed out by this revelation of bizarre eating habits in his own family that he was speechless. He looked at his own knuckles. Even with a baked potato and some string beans thrown in, he knew he'd be hungry half an hour after he ate them.

"Does Sproggy know about Charlie's party?" his mother asked. "Maybe you should call her up and tell her so she won't miss the fun."

"Sproggy knows," he said. He hadn't told his mother about yesterday and his rescue of Sproggy. He liked keeping it to himself awhile. It felt good to be a rescuer of anyone or anything. He had never been one before. He'd tell her sooner or later. In the meantime it was all his.

"Charlie said he might bring his wife Millie over to the building before the party," Adam said. "She's never seen where he works and she'd like to. Plus he told her about the gray lobby and she wants to see for herself. I better get downstairs so I don't miss meeting her."

"Have a lovely time. I'd go with you if I didn't have this creature to subdue." She stirred something in a pot and peered anxiously into its depths. "I simply cannot understand how Julia Child does it," she said. "Imagine talking to that huge audience on TV and cooking at the same time. Absolutely amazing woman, she must be."

When his mother got into this kind of mood, Adam knew, she didn't care whether he stuck around or not. She'd go on talking a mile a minute and stirring her veal knuckle and be perfectly happy. "So long, Mom," he said.

She nodded in his direction, not really seeing him. "I think rice might be nice," she was saying as he left the kitchen. "But, on the other hand . . ."

When Adam got to the lobby, a van had just pulled up outside. A man got out of the driver's seat, ran around to the back, opened the door, and took out a folding wheelchair. He set it on the sidewalk. Charlie got out of the van, reached in, and lifted a woman in his arms.

"Thanks, Herb," he said. "Appreciate it more than I can say."

"My pleasure," Herb said and drove away.

Charlie pushed the woman slowly toward the front door. Adam opened it. "Hi," he said.

"Millie, this here is my friend Adam," Charlie said. "The one I been telling you about all these long years. Adam, this is my wife Millie."

"How do you do?" Millie said, smiling at him. "I've heard so much about you I'm delighted to finally meet you." She put out her hand and Adam took it in his as he would a very small and fragile bird that had fallen from a tree. He was afraid to shake it because it and she looked so frail he thought he might break her bones. On the contrary. Her handclasp was firm and strong. Her voice was rich and hearty and full of life. She sounded just like the woman Adam had pictured in his mind. Underneath her long skirt, he could see her tiny feet dangling from ankles so thin they couldn't possibly have supported her. When she smiled, she showed pointy little teeth, like a child's. Her smile was merry. That much had turned out right, at least. On either side of her mouth was a deep groove, an exaggerated dimple that must have come from years of smiling.

Adam thought he might be able to see through her if the light was right.

I wonder why Charlie didn't tell me about Millie, Adam thought. Probably because she's so happy, such a beautiful person, that Charlie forgets.

As if a silent signal had gone out over the tops of the buildings, saying, "He's here! Charlie's here!" a group of kids, including Steve and Kenny, began to assemble. They milled around, waiting for some action, pretending they didn't know something special was going on.

"Hey!" Charlie said. "It looks like Old Home Week around here." He pushed Millie into the lobby. Adam held open the door and scowled at the rabble on the sidewalk. "Take it easy," he told them. "Don't push, let them breathe." He felt like an usher at Radio City Music Hall, holding back the crowd.

"It's lovely," Millie exclaimed, "such a restful color. I like everything the same color. Very stylish."

"Didn't I tell you?" Charlie said, smiling, his hand on her shoulder. "Like a blinking British pea souper, right?"

The crowd pressed into the lobby. "Everyone, meet my wife Millie!" Charlie called out. "There's more kids in this neighborhood than in any other of the five boroughs, I guess," Charlie said. "They come out of the woodwork.

"And here's the little limey!" Charlie cried as Sproggy appeared.

She was wearing a dress. "Mummy said I had to," she explained to Adam.

"Millie, this here's the little girl from the other side I was telling you about," Charlie said.

"How jolly to meet you," Sproggy said. "When I told Mummy about you being invited to a party at the Mayor's house for educators, she said my Uncle Dickie might be there, too, as he's president of a university in Sussex and should be in New York about this time. You might keep an eye out for him, Charlie. His name's Richard Champion. He's frightfully distinguished looking."

"So's Charlie," Adam said. Everybody stood back and admired Charlie's appearance. He wore a black-and-white checked jacket and a yellow shirt with a red tie. "Isn't he handsome?" Millie said.

"You both are," Adam said, touching upon a streak of gallantry he hadn't known he possessed. Sometimes he surprised himself. Yesterday he'd been kind, today gallant. Who knew what tomorrow might hold?

Charlie kept looking anxiously at his watch. "We don't want to be late," he said. "That would be terrible."

"On the other hand," Millie said, "we don't want to be early either. That would be worse."

"She's got a point," Charlie agreed. "I'm going to push you real slow so you can get a good look at everything." He turned to the crowd. "She doesn't get a chance to see the sights too often, right, Mil?"

"I don't want to miss a thing," Millie said. "And

when I get home tonight, I'm going to write it all down so I won't forget one single detail."

"That's what I do," Sproggy chimed in. "I write in my journal every single night. That way I don't leave out anything. It's very easy to forget when you have so many things happening all at once. That's what I find. I daresay it's the same with you." She and Millie smiled at each other. "Ever since I've come to America, so much has happened to me."

"I hope it's all been good," Millie said.

Sproggy shook her head. "Not all," she said. "Mostly it's been good. But not all."

"That's life," Charlie said. "You got to take the bitter with the sweet, eh?" He started to push Millie in her chair toward their destination. "We'll go across to East End and along the river. You'll like the river, Millie. Always something happening there. And the park's nice. You'll like the park, Mil. And we can stand off and look at that big house and know that in a half hour or so we'll be going there to a party. I don't think too many people have that experience."

Charlie and Millie led the stream of children to the river. Like the Pied Piper, Adam thought. Chattering and laughing, the procession made its way along Eighty-eighth Street, down a couple of blocks to the park. Sure enough, there was a big striped tent set up on the lawn of Gracie Mansion.

"Just look at that!" Millie said. "Imagine! I've

always wanted to go to a party under a tent. What do we say, Charlie, when we're introduced to the Mayor?"

Charlied stopped pushing and became very solemn. "We say, 'How do you do, Your Honor.' That's what they call him. Your Honor."

The entire procession listened, nodded wisely, agreeing with him. It wasn't everyone who knew how to address the Mayor of the city. Looking back, Adam saw they'd picked up some late starters. A couple of women with chins, gloves, and hats asked, "What's this all about?" and a young man in a three-piece suit said, "It's a political rally. Just keep walking." A young couple in blue jeans, with a baby bobbing sleepily on the man's back in a knapsack, joined them happily. Adam imagined how the guard would look if they all followed Charlie and Millie through the gate and up the steps. His face would probably fall apart and he'd call for help on his special line.

"It's almost time," Charlie said nervously. "I think we ought to head over, Mil."

She nodded. "Do I look all right, Charlie? Maybe I should've worn a hat."

He looked at her, studying her. "You'll be the most beautiful woman there. And that's the truth."

"Oh, Charlie!" she said.

"Now you kids behave yourselves," Charlie said. "I want to be proud of all of you. No acting up, no hollering or anything like that. Remember, you're my buddies. If I get a chance, I'll wave."

They nodded. It was a solemn moment. Charlie slowly pushed Millie toward the entrance and the tent and the glowing moment of triumph.

"Bring me a souvenir," Kenny said. "Nothing big or valuable. Just something I can show to my grandchildren."

"You want I should lift one of the Mayor's nightshirts?" Charlie said, grinning.

The children watched as the grownups went through the gate after the guard had inspected their credentials. Adam wondered how Charlie was going to get Millie and her wheelchair up the front steps. They huddled in a small group, faces pressed against the iron fence as if they were peering inside a toy store the week before Christmas.

"I think that's the Mayor shaking hands with Charlie now," Steve said. "It looks like him. There's a bunch of photographers over at the side. What you want to bet Charlie gets on the evening news on TV? I wouldn't be surprised."

Adam watched as a waiter came around with a tray of glasses, which he offered to Millie and Charlie.

"I bet that's champagne," Sproggy said. "It looks like champagne to me." Nobody questioned this. The lawn was filled with ladies and gentlemen. The party was in full swing.

"I wonder how Charlie's getting along," Kenny said.

"All those college presidents and educators."

"Don't worry about Charlie," Adam said. "He can hold his own anywhere."

Sproggy leaned forward, pressing her face against the fence. "I do believe that's Uncle Dickie!" she exclaimed.

"Where?" Necks craned to see Uncle Dickie.

"That tall man in the striped trousers. The one getting out of that huge black car. It certainly looks like him. And Aunt Moggs."

"How can you tell from this far away?"

"Hallo there! Uncle Dickie!" Sproggy's voice rang out in a clarion call. "Hallo!"

Uncle Dickie would have had to be deaf not to hear her, Adam thought, even above the noise of the crowd.

The tall man peered in their direction. He took several steps across the lawn. "Why, Moggs," Adam heard him say, "I do believe that's Sproggy!" He and the lady walked toward the fence, a guard behind them.

"Sproggy, my pet, what are you doing here?" he said.

"Mummy said you might be here," Sproggy said. "How lovely to see you. We"—she made a sweeping gesture to include everybody, including the baby in the knapsack and the two ladies who thought they were attending a political rally—"have a friend who is also at the party. His name is Charlie. He and his wife are going to night school, which is why he was invited. Her name is Millie. She's ever so jolly. I hope you meet them."

"I say," said Uncle Dickie through the fence, "how would it be if I spoke to His Honor and asked if you might be included? He's a good chap, and what's one more guest at a fracas this size?"

"Darling," said Aunt Moggs, "how's Mummy?"

"She's fine, thank you," Sproggy said. "She's settling in very nicely. But, Uncle Dickie, there are such masses of people there, they won't have room for me," she said.

"Precisely," said Uncle Dickie. "What's one more person when there are so many? I say"—he turned to the guard behind him—"would it be possible, do you think, for my god-daughter to attend the party? I haven't seen her in ever so long, and I'm to be in New York only until tomorrow. You'd be doing me such a favor, old boy."

"I'll have to check," the man said. "Wait here," and he went across the lawn and spoke to someone, who spoke to someone else.

The man came back. "His Honor says, 'Fine,' and if the little girl wants to bring a friend, that'll be all right, too."

"Top hole!" Uncle Dickie said. "Thanks, old chap. Come on now, Sproggy, come 'round to the front and bring a chum. I'll be waiting for you there so there won't be any hold-up."

Sproggy clasped her hands. "Oh, Adam," she said, "will you come with me?"

Adam was flabbergasted. In his wildest dreams, and there'd been some pretty wild ones, this is what had happened to him. He had marched up the steps to Gracie Mansion, the warm lights beckoning to him, and had been invited in by the Mayor, and the Mayor's wife had fixed him, with her own hands, a peanut butter sandwich.

"I don't know," he said. Faced with the real thing, he held back.

"Come on!" Sproggy said, taking charge. "We may never have another chance. Besides, we'd better not keep Uncle Dickie waiting."

"Go on, dope," Kenny hissed from behind. "You might miss the whole thing if you don't go now," and he shoved Adam.

"Hey," said the guard, "where you think you're going, buddy? I got no time for you today. There's a big blast going on inside. Lots of bigwigs. Come back tomorrow."

"He's coming with me," Sproggy explained. "There's Uncle Dickie now."

After a few words with the guard, a policeman escorted them all—Adam, Sproggy, and Uncle Dickie—into the party.

Adam's last thought before he lost himself in the excitement of it all was:

Boy, am I glad I wore my new sweater!

The second person he saw was Charlie. The first was the Mayor.

"There you are, Dick. So these are the young people, eh?" The Mayor put out his hand.

Adam had seen his picture so many times he felt as if they were old friends. He shook hands with the Mayor and remembered to say, "Very nice to meet you, sir." He got that "sir" in very well, it seemed to him.

"Awfully good of you to let them come to the party," Uncle Dickie said.

"My pleasure," said the Mayor. "How about some refreshment?"

Adam caught sight of Charlie on his way to the tent. Charlie was talking to a very distinguished-looking man with a goatee.

"Me and my wife Millie are very interested in education," he was saying. "I myself quit school when I was . . . My God!" he said. "What are you doing here, Adam? You better get out before someone catches you."

The distinguished-looking gentleman smiled benignly.

"I'm invited, Charlie," Adam said. "We were watching you through the fence and Sproggy saw her Uncle Dickie and he got the Mayor to ask us in."

"Charming, charming," the distinguished-looking gentleman said. "Such a wonderful country you have.

Where else could something like this happen?"

"Millie," Charlie said, "look who's here."

"I can't believe it," Millie whispered. Adam wasn't sure whether she meant herself or him.

"Me either," said Adam.

"Pardon me," a man said to Charlie, "but are you Charlie Hagelstrom, the handyman who registered for night school classes?"

"That's me," Charlie said proudly.

"Well, we're from Channel Nine's nightly news," the man said. "We'd like to take your picture talking to the Mayor. And your wife too, of course."

Charlie smiled. "That'd be fine with me," he said. "Just let me check with my wife Millie. Millie," he said, bending down to her, "this gentleman wants to put us on Channel Nine's nightly news. That O.K. with you?"

Millie sat up very straight in her chair. She ran a hand over her hair and said, "I think that would be very nice. If it's all right with you, Charlie."

"Why not? It isn't every day we get an opportunity like this. How about the boy, too?" he asked the man.

"Is he a relative of yours?"

"No, he's a friend. A good friend."

The man frowned and said, "I think not, then. Just the two of you. If you don't mind, I'm short on time. Just come over here out of the crowd for a minute and we'll shoot you and the Mayor. Your Honor, would you

144-

be good enough to pose with Mr. Hagelstrom and his wife?"

The Mayor smiled. "It's my pleasure," he said.

Out of the corner of his eye Adam could see Kenny and Steve and the rest of them, faces still pressed against the fence, watching. He stood apart, bowed from the waist, then, straightening, waved both his arms high in the air, acknowledging their presence.

A great roar arose from the watchers.

"Yeh," they cried, "yeh, yeh, yeh!" Then "Hip hip hooray!" they shouted.

"Now, Your Honor, if you'll just smile at Mr. and Mrs. Hagelstrom," the TV cameraman said, "and say a few words."

"It's a great pleasure for me to welcome such fine people to Gracie Mansion on such a wonderful day in such a wonderful city," the Mayor said. "It's people like Mr. and Mrs. Hagelstrom that make this country of ours what it is."

The Mayor was notoriously long-winded. He made a speech about how the Hagelstroms' desire for further education epitomized the spirit of special Continuing Education Week and was in the best American tradition. The TV cameraman began to twitch nervously.

"Thank you, Your Honor," he said several times. Finally the Mayor finished. Everyone shook everyone else's hand.

"Good-bye, Uncle Dickie and Aunt Moggs,"

Sproggy cried, throwing her arms about them both. "Mummy will be so sorry to have missed you."

"We'll be in New York again in a few months," Aunt Moggs said. "We'll see you all then."

"Good show!" Uncle Dickie said.

"I've got to get home to watch the nightly news," Adam said.

"Me, too," Charlie said. "Thank you, Your Honor, for a most memorable day. The most memorable day in me and Millie's life. We'll never forget it."

The Mayor said he felt the same way—although he must have had many memorable days in his life, Adam thought.

"Your car is ready whenever you are, Mr. Hagelstrom," the Mayor's aide said.

"Our car!" Charlie looked stunned.

The man opened the door of a long, gleaming limousine. "We would have sent one for you and your wife to bring you to Gracie Mansion, but no one answered your telephone last night," the aide said.

"We were playing Bingo," Charlie explained. "That's all right. Herb brought us over."

The driver tipped his hat. "We'd better leave now if you folks want to catch yourselves on the nightly news," he said. Charlie lifted Millie in his arms and put her in the wide back seat. Then he got in beside her as the driver folded Millie's chair and put it in the trunk.

146-

"Good-bye, Charlie and Millie!" everyone hollered. "Good-bye and happy landings!" The limousine pulled out of the drive and into East End Avenue, headed for Charlie's house. The neighbors, Adam felt sure, would be there, waiting when the Hagelstroms arrived home, celebrities, TV stars, everything.

Kenny, his face marked where he'd rested it against the iron fence, came running as he saw Adam and Sproggy walking toward him.

"How'd it go?" he said. "How was it? Did you meet the Mayor? Who else was there? Did you get on TV?"

"Listen," Adam said, very cool and collected, "if you want to catch Charlie and Millie on the nightly news, you'd better hotfoot it for home on account of they're on at six."

"No kidding?" Steve's eyes bugged. Even *he* was impressed, and it took a whole lot to impress Steve. "What'd he do to get on?"

"He registered for night school courses is what he did."

"As simple as that, eh?" Steve shook his head. "I bet everybody he knows is going to rush out and do the same so they can get invited to a party at Gracie Mansion and wind up on TV."

"Did you see us?" Adam asked casually. "We were standing around chewing the fat with all the big shots. Did you see us?"

"Yeah, we saw you," Kenny said. "It didn't look like you were doing much talking. I didn't see your mouth move once, if you want to know. Only when you were eating. Every time the waiter came by with a tray, I saw your old mitt whip out and take something off that tray. That's the only time I saw your mouth move, when you were chomping on the food. What'd you have to eat—caviar?"

"Caviar? What's that?" Adam asked.

"Fish eggs," Kenny said.

"Fish eggs? You gotta be kidding me!" Adam said.

"Oh, I don't think there was any caviar," Sproggy said. "I wish there had been. I absolutely love caviar."

"Whew!" Adam wiped his forehead. The idea of fish eggs swimming around his insides made him very uncomfortable.

"I can hardly wait to write and tell Wendy about it," Sproggy said. "I must go home this minute and write to her before I forget anything. Good-bye. I'll see you all tomorrow," and she hurried off, taking giant steps so she'd get home before her memory failed.

They watched her go. "If it wasn't for *her*," Steve said, poking a grimy finger at Adam's chest, "you wouldn't have got inside."

"Give me a break," Adam said. "I know that. I better head for home too so I don't miss the news." He took off. Sproggy was already out of sight.

Just as he opened the door, the phone rang.

"Hello," his father's voice said. "Just wanted to wish you good luck on your first day of school tomorrow and ask you if you'd like to go on the Staten Island ferry on Saturday. Take a ride over and back and maybe go to the Statue of Liberty. How does that sound?" his father said. "Just you and me."

"Sure, Dad," Adam said. "Let's take Sproggy along too."

There was a silence as his father digested this turn of events.

"Sproggy? Certainly. I'd be delighted to have her along. If you're sure . . ."

"Dad, I've got to turn on the TV," Adam said. "Watch the nightly news on Channel Nine. Charlie's on. My friend Charlie who works in the building. I've gotta go. See you," and Adam hung up and raced to turn on the set.

"What's going on?" Adam's mother asked. "What's all the commotion?"

Adam put his finger to his lips. "Watch!" he said.

"At a party this afternoon at Gracie Mansion," the announcer said, "there were many guests—college presidents and educators all over the world. And also attending were Charlie Hagelstrom and his wife Millie."

Adam and his mother watched in silence as Charlie said a few words, the sun shining on him and Millie and the Mayor.

"Ma," Adam hissed, "you see that arm in the back? That red arm? That's me."

"What?" she said.

"Wait'll Charlie gets finished and I'll tell you," he said. "I and Sproggy were there."

CHAPTER 17

After school on Monday Adam sped home, anxious to see Charlie. He found him waxing the lobby floor. Adam sat down and waited for Charlie to finish.

"Mind the corners, Charlie," the super said, standing in the doorway. "I had a couple complaints lately."

Charlie shut off the waxer. "I'd like to know the name of the individuals who complained," he said. "I pride myself on always doing a good job."

"Hey, all I said was mind the corners." The super backed off. "Just because you're a celebrity, a TV star, don't go and get a swelled head on me." He smiled his joyless smile.

"Charlie would never get a swelled head," Adam said.

"Just mind your p's and q's and everything will be jake," the super said and disappeared.

"That guy," Charlie said. "One of nature's misfits. A totally unhappy guy. Never satisfied, always nitpicking. If Santa Claus came down his chimney with a full load of presents, he'd say, 'Watch them ashes, big boy.' " Charlie shook his head. "Mind the corners," he muttered. "These are the cleanest corners in the whole city." He finished polishing and sat down.

"You want a pickle?" he asked Adam, opening his lunch box. "Millie made 'em. Beat any deli pickle I ever ate."

Adam accepted gratefully. "Tell me about yesterday," he said. "What happened when the limo took you home. I bet your neighbors flipped out."

"It was beautiful, beautiful." Charlie put his head back and closed his eyes, smiling blissfully. "There was a band—a couple of guys on the block play sax, trombone, even a cello. They were waiting, and when the chauffeur opened the door for us, they broke into 'For He's a Jolly Good Fellow.'

"That did it," Charlie said, sitting up straight. "Millie cried. She went all to pieces, she was so happy. And if you want to know, I teared up some myself. Oh, it was grand. Me and Millie agreed it was the high spot in our lives.

"Then our friends brought over a turkey and a ham and some casseroles composed of unknown but tasty ingredients, and we made the welkin ring."

"What's 'welkin' mean?" Adam asked.

Charlie knit his brow. "I don't exactly know," he admitted, "but whatever it is, we made it ring. I read that in a book once, and I been meaning to look it up, but I keep forgetting. It's a good word. I never had a chance to use it before but that time it fit right in." Charlie looked pleased with himself.

"You want to know the conclusion I came to after that gala affair yesterday?" he asked Adam, who nodded.

"I came to the conclusion that the true test of greatness is in how the big man treats the little guy, the low man on the totem pole, like me and Millie. They treat him like he was the Shah of Iran, not to mention a college president. Here I am, a thirteen-year-old school dropout, mingling with the hoi polloi. That joint was jammed with *summa cums* and Ph.D.'s, all that business, and they treated us just as nice." Charlie shook his head in wonder. "Me and Millie couldn't get over it. Just because I got on a shirt and tie doesn't mean I got one quarter the gray matter them boys have rattling around inside their heads. But nobody woulda known I was any different. It's enough to restore man's faith in his fellow man.

"Do you want another pickle?" Charlie dipped into

his supply and came up with two more.

"Me and Millie were tickled pink to see you and the little limey girl getting along like a house afire," Charlie said, leaning over to catch the pickle juice in his hand. "Nice she got you invited to the party. Now you're friends for life, eh?"

"We were friends before that," Adam said. "It wasn't because she got me into the party that made us friends," he added defensively. He didn't want Charlie thinking *that*.

"What did?" Charlie asked.

"Well," Adam said slowly, "I think it was because I found out she wasn't such a hotshot after all. I mean, she needed someone to stand up for her, and I stood up. I was kind to her. That isn't what *I* said," he added hastily, not wanting Charlie to get the wrong idea. "That's what she said. A bunch of clods were making fun of her, and she couldn't handle it, and I stood up for her."

Charlie put his hands on Adam's shoulders. "Hey," he said, "you are an humanitarian, just like you said. I'm proud of you, Adam. Overnight, practically, you become an humanitarian. Not too many people can boast of that. You cast your bread upon the waters and it comes up roses, so to speak. Good work."

Adam tried to look modest.

"It wasn't so much," he said.

Charlie pulled his dustcloth out of his back pocket and went to work.

"No," he agreed, "but every little bit helps."

"It wasn't easy, though," Adam said hastily, not wanting to turn off Charlie's admiration. "As a matter of fact, it was pretty hard."

Charlie began to whistle "For He's a Jolly Good Fellow," and when he caught Adam's eye, they both began to laugh.